ANNIE ARCHER PARANORMAL MYSTERIES

VOLUME ONE

DAISY LANDISH

Editing by Rachael Lammie
Cover by Daisy Landish

BEACHES AND TRAILS
PUBLISHING

CONTENTS

THE CASE OF THE DEADLY TRUFFLES

THE CASE OF THE MISSING MILLIONS

THE CASE OF THE MISSING COFFIN

THE CASE OF THE UNLUCKY HANDYMAN

THE CASE OF THE AMETHYST PENDANT

AN ANNIE ARCHER PARANORMAL MYSTERY

THE CASE OF THE

DEADLY TRUFFLES

A COZY MYSTERY

DAISY LANDISH

CHAPTER ONE

WITCHES, generally speaking, are not typically known for being kind and generous. Often depicted as hunched over crones cursing children or mystical old women doling out cryptic advice to passers-by, witches tend to be feared rather than loved.

Annie Archer, however, considered herself the exception to this rule. Indeed, Annie Archer was a 'good witch'.

When she first got to Turtle Bay and started her new job as a security agent, she wasn't sure how she'd be able to put her more supernatural abilities to good use. Sure, she could do little things here and there–like offering her neighbor a tonic she made when she noticed his painful, hacking cough. He'd gotten better in less than a day, and she preened a little internally, knowing she was responsible for his recovery.

Annie needed some good deeds in her life. If she were completely honest, her life had been too hectic, too stressful. Until now. Living in the city had knotted her up in ways she couldn't begin to untangle. Moving became the only answer that made sense. She needed a slower pace. A chance to enjoy becoming part of a community, and fitting in. In short, she craved the small-town life, which looked so appealing in every Hallmark movie she pretended to loathe.

She wanted a fresh start. A new beginning.

But so far, small-town life hadn't exactly solved all her problems. Since she had packed herself up and started a new life in Turtle Bay, she had discovered the problem wasn't entirely the fault of her setting. Annie found it hard to relax.

Annie supposed it was because she was still recovering from her recent divorce. It wasn't an amicable split. She refused to take the blame for what happened though. She wasn't the type of woman to beg for a man's attention, so when she'd found out her husband was telling everyone he preferred blondes (Annie had naturally dark hair) and 'pliable' women, she asked for a divorce. Who could blame her? The very fact he'd made those statements while flirting with a very available woman had been the last straw. Oh sure, he'd put up some protests initially, but once he was sure she was serious, he caved and signed the papers.

She would feel freer, younger, and hopefully happier as a single woman. Five years of her life had been wasted loving and caring for a man who'd never really held up his end of the "to love and to cherish" part of their wedding vows.

Her husband's proclivities notwithstanding, Annie realized there would be little to miss. While she was constantly trying to improve his life, health, and home, her ex was never fully present for her. In the end, they'd lived almost as though they'd been amicable roommates with the occasional 'benefits'. His cheating had almost been a relief, an excuse to end something that had been dragging on far too long already.

She decided she would refocus that energy toward her new job and life in Turtle Bay.

When she met Sheriff Parker, her purpose became crystal clear. She was meant to help the police solve cases. It was ironic as she'd tried to get into the police academy without success. Now, here she was assisting a Sheriff with his most challenging cases without having to go through the rigorous training and the life of a beat cop. Sure, it wasn't a paid gig, but it was fulfilling in many other ways.

For one thing, she enjoyed the problem-solving aspect of her work immensely. With her acting as a special consultant to the Sheriff's office, they worked around her schedule, and she rarely had to miss work. Best of all, Sheriff Parker treated her with respect and valued her input and gifts.

Annie used her powers, and the odd potion, to confuse the perpetrator and lead them into the trap the police would have set for them. She and Sheriff Parker worked well together. He had recently requested she start calling him Adam. He respected her unique gifts and appreciated her creative approach. Privately, he told her that he sometimes found traditional investigative methods reductive and not all that effective. This had made Annie smile, and he gave her a conspiratorial wink. Annie liked that they had a private joke, and she liked having Adam as a friend.

Adam had been a great resource in kicking off her new life. He had introduced her to his circle of friends, and her integration into the community had been assured. His endorsement went a long way in soothing Annie's worries. People often had mixed reactions when they found out she had 'special' gifts. Either they were awed and asked for readings or seances, or they thought she was nuts or, worse, a charlatan.

Life went on. Anne worked her day job, volunteering during her time off, and always assisted Sheriff Parker when he called. She'd never turned him down. And frankly, never had plans to start.

Lately, though, it had become challenging to let go and enjoy her new life. She'd been having visions about the cases they worked together. Well, that in itself wasn't unusual. What was worrisome to Annie was that these visions came to her *while she was awake.*

One troublesome question continued to roam Annie's mind. *Where do these visions come from?* No one in her family had similar gifts that she knew of. She felt it was rather disconcerting to see events as they occurred. Usually, this kind of vision came in dreams when she was deeply asleep. Not during the day, and not as events were happening.

To be fair, I've had strange visions before, she thought as she stared at the ghost who attempted to watch TV in her living room. Lately, he had taken to reality shows. It annoyed her endlessly; particularly since she'd found a way to cast a spell on the remote so he could use it to turn on the TV at will. She'd quickly realized her mistake when the TV came on at 3:00 a.m. at full volume one night. It brought her instantly awake, heart racing, and trying to figure out just how the world was coming to an end.

No, Monty wasn't the problem. Ghosts weren't visions, just occasional roommates. Visions were something else altogether.

She thought back to the latest investigation she worked on, led by Sheriff Adam Parker. Annie had seen the alleged victim, alive and well, and trying to flee the country – *before* – the events occurred. Her premonition helped solve the case. But it had been unsettling in a new way. After the fact, Adam had asked her if she was okay, and she assured him she was. She hoped she would be, but now she was not so sure.

A glimpse of the past seemed simple. And things going on in real-time presented too much immediacy, creating awful stress as she tried to sort out what she could possibly do about what she saw. But seeing things that were *about* to happen? This level of visioning was almost too much. It called into question whether the future was set in stone or was something that could be changed. There were philosophical questions here, which she couldn't begin to unravel.

Not that Annie wasn't grateful for this added gift, but doubt gnawed at her gut. She was not an anxious woman by nature. But something felt different about this addition to her repertoire of witchy talents and abilities. She'd never heard of any witch alive today having waking visions unless they were a harbinger of doom or a soothsayer. And Annie didn't consider herself either one of those things.

She paced her house that afternoon, finally driving Monty crazy enough that he gave up on the TV and went to hide in the attic. Just as well because Annie needed to think, and the elaborate charades, which made up the bulk of their communication, were exhausting to say the least. Alone, she turned the conundrum over in her mind, trying to rationalize this sudden new development. After a few hours of pacing, Annie started to worry about her health. What if she messed something up in one of her spells or potions? Was this an indication of a more serious internal issue? What if she had made some horrible mistake, and this was nothing more than a really unpleasant side effect?

She shuddered at the thought. With unease rolling through her, she phoned her coven sister, Rosemary. The latter had been like a mentor to Annie after her mother passed away. Rosemary had taught Annie most of the spells and curses Annie used and even some that she wouldn't dare use. Rosemary was older than her, in her 50s, and wasn't the sort to be bothered by spontaneous phone calls.

Besides, she might not even answer if she's really deep in her spell work.

Reassured somewhat, Annie dialed the number before she lost her nerve.

The line rang several times before Rosemary picked up. Ever the observant, Rosemary seemed to know Annie needed to talk about something serious before she even got a word out. "What's wrong?"

Her kindness almost undid her. Rosemary encouraged Annie to explain what got her worked up, and so she did in great detail.

"And you're saying that you have premonitions while you're awake?" Rosemary asked once Annie had explained what happened in the previous week.

"Yes. That's exactly what I'm saying. And I'd like to find out where these visions come from, or if someone has slipped something into my tea, so to speak." Annie sat down heavily at her kitchen table and fiddled with the teacup she'd left sitting there that morning.

Rosemary was quiet as she considered this. "I think you've got something there, Annie. You must have consumed some hallucinogen, which has provided you with instant mind-travel," Rosemary paused. "As I understand it, you saw the lady while she called 9-1-1 saying that she was being attacked – as if you were right there. Is that correct dear?"

Annie nodded to herself and said out loud, "Yes. I actually thought I had been there in that garden somehow. It all felt so real!"

Annie could almost picture Rosemary nodding at her, lips pursed, a self-satisfied look in her eyes, the way she did when one of her theories had been confirmed. "Exactly. The only thing I can suggest is that you buy new herbs and teas for your potions and new spices for cooking. I suspect someone slipped something into your pantry."

With that, Rosemary hung up abruptly, leaving Annie floundering on the other end. She set the phone down and sat back in her chair, thinking about who could've had access to her food or drinks. Or her house, for that matter. And why would they potentially infest her herbs and spices? She kicked herself internally for not suspecting such a thing in the first place. Annie tended to blame herself before putting any blame on others.

Her ex had told her once that she was too naive, too gullible. Maybe he had a point. But she could argue that she'd rather be sure of the good in people than be on the lookout for the bad. This time, however, she needed to consider the alternative. Certain people in the world liked to make mischief for others. She figured she would have to at least consider that someone might have it out for her specifically.

She shouted for Monty to see if he could try to shed any light on the subject. But he was still ignoring her apparently. Monty had so far proven to be a taciturn companion, showing up with about the reliability of a cat. So far, her efforts to make friends had fallen flat, despite her assistance with the TV remote. She would ask him about visitors later, she decided. In the meantime, she better get down to work.

Heeding her mentor's words, Annie realized that she was going to have to empty every cupboard in her kitchen and every shelf in her pantry. She grabbed the trash can for easy access and a step stool so she could reach her higher shelves. Before she started, she sighed and hung her head. She put so much work into her stockpile of supplies. It was kind of disheartening to have to dismantle it all based on a hunch.

What a waste, she thought. *I'll have to spend a mere fortune to replace all of these herbs –if I can even replace all of them.* Some of them were rare.

Carefully, she removed jar after jar of herbs, spices, and tiny samples of various things, including insect wings, bee pollen, cat hair, and dried-up fruits. She lined the jars upon the table until it was packed to the edges with her wares. Sighing, she opened the jars one by one and dumped the contents into the trash. The different smells that hit her nose were comforting. She gave each jar one last sniff before discarding her efforts. She hoped the men who picked up the trash wouldn't be too grossed out. She pressed on, dumping out jars, rinsing them clean, then going at it again. Within an hour, she knew this task would take the remainder of the day, and she groaned internally.

When she was filling her second garbage bag full of discarded items, the phone rang. Annie wiped her hands on a tea towel and picked up the receiver just as Monty manifested himself and started perusing the jars lined up on the counter.

"Annie speaking," she said before the caller could identify herself.

"Ms. Archer, this is Adeline Carmel. I've just opened the flower shop on Garden Street, and I was wondering if you would like to come in for our grand opening."

A flower shop? Annie thought about some of the dried herbs and flowers she had literally just discarded. It seemed perfect.

Perhaps a little *too* perfect?

Monty was mouthing something at her, pointing from the phone to the jars and back again. His fingers flew in a mixture of sign language and gestures.

A trap.

He didn't need to say the rest, for she'd been thinking the same thing. Either this was incredible timing, which given the nature of her witchcraft, could be explained as certain forces trying to make right some of her losses. Or this was something more sinister, as Monty implied, created by the very person who had messed with her supplies in the first place.

She waved at Monty, letting him know she'd seen him and to let her talk. "Ms. Carmel, may I ask who gave you my phone number?"

CHAPTER TWO

"OH GOODNESS, didn't I say? Sheriff Parker gave me your number." Ms. Carmel chuckled as though this conversation was the most amusing thing she'd experienced all day. "We chatted the other day about security. I mentioned that I would like to invite some of the women in the community for the opening day of my new shop. That's when he mentioned your name. He thought you might be interested in attending."

Annie rolled her eyes at Monty who silently snickered. She didn't like the idea of being slotted in with the "women of the community," especially given that she kept somewhat to herself. Without knowing the locals all that well, it was hard to know whether being lumped in with them would be considered a good thing or a bad thing.

But what the heck, she thought finally, thinking her ex was making her too suspicious. *I'll meet some new people, which I've been needing to do since I moved. What harm could there possibly be in that?*

"Thank you, Ms. Carmel. If you give me a date and time, I'll make sure to be there," Annie said, picking at her nails while she talked, trying to work out some bits of herbs, which had caught under her nails in the cleaning process.

"That's marvelous!" Adeline exclaimed and started to rattle off details.

Annie abandoned her nails and quickly got out a pen and paper to jot down the date and time for the party. Once these details were shared though, Ms. Carmel ended the call abruptly, leaving Annie a little puzzled. The woman had seemed so friendly at the start of the call. Had she done something to offend her to make her hang up so quickly?

"I suspect she just wanted to move on to the next call," she said finally, shaking her head. "Isn't it weird," she wondered aloud as she went back to her work of dumping jars of carefully collected supplies into the garbage, "that he gave her my personal number without asking me first?"

Monty seemed to agree. He was bent over the trash can, expression unreadable as he examined what she'd been throwing out. Annie wondered what he was thinking. Odd as it sounded, she valued Monty's opinion.

Monty was somewhat stuffy about things. But so far, he seemed to have her best interests at heart. He had shown himself about a week after she'd moved in. He seemed to have difficulty speaking but given the obvious injury to his neck, maybe this made a weird sort of sense. She'd tried to research him, but she hadn't found any local legends about any 200-year-old ghosts in the neighborhood. She started calling him Monty because her house was on Montgomery Street and he didn't seem to mind. For all she knew, the street was named after him.

Annie spotted a shadow outside and looked out to see a crow perched on her fence. Crows could be an omen. Though for all she knew, this bird might just be hungry and attracted to the smell of the items she was emptying into the trash. She brushed it off as a coincidence and went back to her work. There was certainly still enough of it to do. Annie surveyed the table and sighed. It would be a long afternoon. "Want to help?" she smiled at Monty, knowing full well how difficult it was for him to pick things up.

He grimaced and disappeared. She heard the TV click on.

"Thanks, Monty. I appreciate you SOOOO much..." she muttered and dug back into work.

It was well-beyond nightfall by the time Annie was done. She decided to leave the clean jars on the table to dry and to fill again when she could get out to buy more supplies. She sat down to make a list and inwardly groaned; this would be a huge shopping trip. She wasn't even sure she could find everything she needed without going to a big city.

Goldenseal
Lavender Sprig
Celtic Sea Salt
Dried Hibiscus Blossoms
Dried Rose Petals
Dried Oregano Leaves
Caraway Seeds
Dried Star Anise
Wormwood
Dandelion Root
Stinging Nettle
Spearmint

Annie paused reading her list and sighed. Maybe she should stick with whatever would be enough to get her started. She could spot most of the other items she needed when she got to a proper store. So long as she made sure her heavy hitters were present and accounted for, she would be ok.

Annie missed the spearmint dearly when she went to make her nightly cup of tea. She made do with a less flavorful cup of tea from an unopened box of tea bags she found in the pantry and sat down with a book to read by lamplight. Monty had given up on the TV and the house was quiet for once. Despite the phone call earlier, which had rattled her considerably, it had turned out to be a lovely evening. The book she was reading was different from her usual fare. This particular author wrote romance-type novels where the heroine gets swept off her feet by a dashing rogue who whisks her away from her dull life. While Annie liked her life, there was nothing wrong with a bit of wishing now and again, she reasoned.

An hour later, her eyes started to feel droopy. She went around the house one last time to check the door and window locks. Just to be safe, she placed a few wards, charms really, to assure no one could enter the house without her knowledge and turned off the lights as she usually did. Typically, she wasn't a paranoid witch. Still, Annie slept a little better that night, knowing she was locked in safely and securely. She shortly fell into a fitful sleep, her body carrying over her worry once her mind had quieted.

The next day, she went to see Sheriff Parker in his office. Usually, she would be chipper and happy to start the day with him. But she was still a little miffed that he was potentially giving out her personal information. But he also seemed chipper, and his smile immediately put her in a good mood, making it hard to complain exactly. She couldn't resist a little jab, though, so she said, "Thanks for giving my phone number to Ms. Carmel." She chuckled and shook her head. "Are you going to be there too?"

Adam stopped what he was doing and folded his arms. His eyebrows scrunched as if he was thinking hard, and he frowned before he asked, "Huh? Be where?"

Annie was caught off-guard by his question. She felt the hair on her arms stand up, a sure-fire sign something was amiss. Another crow outside cawed rather ominously. It sounded as though it said, "beware."

"Ms. Carmel? The new owner of the flower shop on Garden Street? She phoned me yesterday. She wanted to invite me to the grand opening. She said she got my number from you."

"From me?" Adam was already shaking his head, vehement in his denial. "I don't recall being invited, nor do I recall talking to a Ms. Carmel."

He took off his glasses. Adam was now sitting up at his desk, giving her a puzzled and concerned look. She felt a little embarrassed, not wanting him to worry. It was just the grand opening of a store after all, hardly anything threatening. Wasn't it? All the same, she was quick to shrug off the entire matter, not wanting to alert Adam to her suspicions just yet. "In any case, the lady obtained my phone number from someone and is expecting me to be at her grand opening on Saturday. Can you make it?"

Deep down, she was wishing her friend would be free to accompany her. Now that she knew this woman had her number and might therefore know where she lived, she'd feel better if she wasn't going into unknown territory all on her own. Just in case this wasn't just some store promotion but something else entirely.

Adam looked briefly at his desk calendar before he answered. "Sure. It will allow me to see just who's invoking my name to get to you." He pulled out a pen and made a note on the edge of a piece of paperwork. "I'll run a check on Ms. Carmel in the meantime and let you know if anything untoward pops up. Okay?"

Annie gave him a smile and a nod, somehow managing to laugh lightly when she said, "Glad to hear that someone other than me is going to keep you on your toes."

Adam laughed and shrugged his shoulders. It was clear he wanted to get back to work for he was already returning to the paperwork he was filling out. Annie watched him for a moment, noting how his mouth twitched when he was thinking, how he bit the pen when he was in between written words.

She decided not to bother him anymore and waved goodbye cheerfully as though she hadn't a care in the world.

In truth, she was troubled. And she was wondering if there was some spell she might cast, which would give her a little clarity about the whole matter. She thought about this as she went about her own work for the day, making sure to keep the Sheriff's office in her line of sight. Talking about the conversation with Ms. Carmel had her a little on edge, and though she knew she could defend herself, if need be, it never hurt to have the law on her side. Especially when the law was held up by such a good guy like Sheriff Parker.

Adam showed up at the end of her shift to walk her to her car like he did every night since the days had grown shorter. She'd told him countless times that he didn't have to just because it was dark out, but he insisted regardless. Still somewhat bemused by the way he fussed over her, she got into her little yellow car and shut the door. Adam leaned next to her rolled-down window and said, "You get home safe now, Annie. Okay?"

It was sweet that he cared, but she wasn't altogether sure what he was so worried about. Turtle Bay was hardly a hotbed of crime, and if you ever met another car on Main Street at this hour, you'd be surprised.

Annie nodded, and he waved her off. In the rear-view mirror, she noticed that he watched her until she was out of sight instead of turning around and going back into the building like he usually did. *Best not read too much into that,* she thought. *He was probably just being nice.*

She went about her evening like normal and didn't think of Ms. Carmel again that night. Annie stayed up late to finish her book since she didn't have to work the next day and sighed when the story ended happily, just as she predicted it would.

That night, she dreamt of a handsome man taking her in his arms and kissing her senseless. His face looked vaguely familiar. When she woke up, she decided not to dwell on it. Not everything was a sign, after all, nor was meant to have deep meaning ascribed to it. If the Sheriff showed up in her dreams, it was merely because she'd spent time with him yesterday.

Shopping was on her agenda for the day, especially since she'd planned on baking some bread and maybe renting a movie to watch later that night. Maybe she could talk Monty into watching with her.

Since Annie woke with the sun most days, today was no different. She considered how easily she could get these tasks done during the day. But she lingered. She took her time drinking her coffee and selecting her outfit. She wanted to savor the day, not rush through it. Otherwise, she'd be living exactly as she had back when she'd resided in Boston, always hurrying about.

Slow down today. You have all the time in the world, even if you have a lot going on.

After some debate, Annie decided on denim overalls with a white linen shirt underneath and boots that were comfortable enough to walk in. She threw on a sunhat, since the weather looked bright and cheery, and headed out the door with reusable bags and baskets in tow, ready for a long day with an even longer to-do list.

Her first stop was a plant nursery. She needed a rosemary plant to keep in the kitchen, a few dozen fresh-cut roses to dry out, and some locally sourced basil. The nursery owner was a kind older man whose wife passed away last year. He tipped his cap to Annie as she entered, and he personally rang her up when she was ready to leave.

"Any chance you need some spearmint too?" he asked as he packed up her things. "Got a fresh pallet in this morning but haven't had the chance to put it out."

"Oh my gosh, yes!" Annie exclaimed, thinking sometimes things worked out rather serendipitously. "I do need some if you don't mind." He gave her two for the price of one, confiding in her that she was his favorite customer when she tried to give him money for the second spearmint plant.

"Thank you," Annie said sincerely, reaching out to clasp the man's hand. She hadn't been there long enough to be his favorite anything, but the sentiment was kind. Thinking one good turn deserved another, she silently recited a spell for prosperity in her mind before she released his hand. He grinned at her and waved as she left.

Her next few stops were all on Garden Street, so she parked at one end and made her way down. She visited an herbalist shop, had a quick bite at a cafe, and picked up some baking supplies. She also got a few jars of local honey from the town beekeeper.

While passing down the opposite side of Garden Street, she looked at the new flower shop whose windows were decorated with satin drapes and purple organza under impressive crystal vases. People were bustling in and out of the new establishment. With so much activity, the shop was positively buzzing.

Wow, Ms. Carmel is going all out for her new shop, she mused, a smile gracing her lips. Maybe the store's grand opening wouldn't be so bad after all.

Feeling well-satisfied with how her errands had turned out, Annie decided she was done for the day and headed back to her car to go home.

Funny. After observing the hustle and bustle she'd seen at the new shop, she should have been more reassured about Ms. Carmel's invitation. But the more she thought about it, the more unease started to climb her throat again. Why would this woman, who clearly had better things to worry about, be *so* adamant that Annie attend the grand opening?

She knew she'd have to find out.

CHAPTER THREE

ONCE SHE HAD DROPPED her purchases at home, Annie decided to go to her office to see if she could learn a few more things about Ms. Carmel. She'd debated about going in at all. She was technically working from home, which allowed her to start work any time of day she wanted, but she didn't have all the resources she thought she might need in her little house.

She made herself a sandwich for lunch first and sat down at her table to eat while she considered her next move. The kitchen was cluttered now, with the cleaned-out jars and bags of new supplies, so she had to carve out a spot amid all the rest. She told herself that a little food in her stomach would help her concentrate. Besides, she didn't want to go to work only to have to leave for lunch and then come back again afterward. The more she came and went, the more likely she would be spotted by her co-workers, not to mention anyone else who might be watching her.

Nope, better to be in and out quickly and quietly, she decided. After her meal, she got back in her little yellow car and drove away, her mind wandering back to the events of the past few days concerning Ms. Carmel.

Although she appreciated Adam checking into the strange

woman's background, Annie still didn't like the idea that Ms. Carmel had lied to her about obtaining her phone number from Adam. The fact that this woman knew to drop his name as one Annie would trust was disconcerting.

She slipped into work a little after twelve when most of the department would be on lunch or out on patrol. She carefully and quietly got to work, rummaging through some files, and taking notes. With a glance at the clock, Annie decided she wouldn't need more than a few hours to get what she needed. Then, hopefully, she could sneak out again, unnoticed.

Her afternoon didn't exactly go as planned.

"What are you doing here?" Mr. Strauss, her boss, asked as he poked his head in the doorway of Annie's office. His sudden intrusion caused her to jump and drop the file she was holding. He raised his eyebrows quizzically, and she huffed as she gathered her materials from the floor.

"I thought you were working from home on the Callister case?" he asked, watching her scramble about picking up bits of paper. Annie raised her face to him and shrugged, "And I am. But I came across something that bothered me. I wanted to check that a certain lady has all of her business permits in order."

Her reasoning made Strauss pause. He was a nice enough man, and he was very professional, if not a little stuffy. But he trusted Annie's judgment, meaning if she was worried, he would be all ears. At least that's what she hoped.

"Who are we talking about," Strauss asked, stepping into Annie's office.

"Ms. Adeline Carmel and her new flower shop on Garden Street," she replied, finally situating her paperwork enough to settle back down at her desk.

Strauss raised both eyebrows. "Strange that you ask," he said, taking a seat across from Annie. "She's been asking the mayor to make an appearance at her grand opening, and he phoned earlier this morning with the same queries as yours."

Annie settled back comfortably in her desk chair, leaning back further as she considered this. "And I bet he said that she obtained Mr. Davidson's number from you?"

Strauss blinked at her, seemingly surprised.

Annie snapped forward, leaning so that she might place her elbows on the desk. "She claims that she got my number from Adam Parker. And he says he doesn't even know the woman."

They both sat still and thought for a moment, then suddenly Mr. Strauss seemed to remember he had other things to attend to. "Okay then," Strauss said, getting to his feet. "Something is definitely up. I've organized a security detail for Mr. Davidson, and I'd like you to coordinate with Adam on this – so that we don't end up with a dead mayor, or whatever else the woman is planning to attempt."

A dead mayor? Annie was caught off guard. She hadn't considered anything quite so nefarious. At the same time, she was glad that someone was taking her concern as seriously as she was. In this case, Annie agreed with the extra precautions. *An ounce of prevention is better than a pound of cure.* Hadn't her grandmother taught her that?

Her boss left her office with a reminder that she better get home before other people realized she was there and started asking for her help. She laughed as he retreated and got back to her search. It didn't take her long to verify that Ms. Carmel's permits and building inspections were legally obtained and carried out in a normal manner. She put the permits back in the appropriate folders and went home to get her purchases sorted and unpacked. She'd be glad for the peace and quiet so she could think more through her next action plan.

That night was her weekly dinner "date" with Sheriff Parker, and he arrived right on time. Monty answered the door. Well, he arrived there first. Annie gave him a warning look before putting her hand on the doorknob.

"Behave tonight, okay?"

Monty shrugged. His grin put her off a bit. Malicious? Or just mischievous. She ignored him and flung open the door. "I'm so glad you came!" she said by way of greeting, as though he wasn't there just about every week.

"How are you, my little witch?" he asked, giving her a brief hug. Any lingering doubts she had over whether he could sense the ghost were dispelled when he walked right through Monty as he followed her to the kitchen.

Monty scowled and winked out. Annie hoped he'd stay out for the night. The ghost manifested as someone old enough to be her grandfather. Hardly the face she wanted to be looking at if she wound up cuddling on the couch with the Sheriff after dinner. Not that they really cuddled exactly.

Yet.

As busy as she had been all day, Annie hadn't quite managed to put everything quite to rights again. Still, she'd managed to make a nice dinner and the kitchen looked fairly normal to her eyes. She found herself really looking forward to the night as they sat down to dinner, enjoying that she could laugh and joke with her guest and let go of her worries about the day.

They ate Annie's famous beef stew, and Adam seemed relaxed, more than usual. He didn't bring up work once while they ate. Instead, he told her all about the new TV show he was watching. He was helping her clear the table when he asked if she'd gotten new spice jars or just new spices.

Annie followed his gaze to the row of empty jars sitting next to the sink, which she hadn't filled yet, and felt herself grow warm at his question. *He'd noticed that? How interesting.* "Just doing a little cleaning and restock," she half-lied. No need to worry him about the strange things she'd been going through, or her suspicions that Ms. Carmel was linked to these incidents quite yet. Especially when they hadn't even spoken to the woman face-to-face.

She changed the subject to ask him about some detail about the show they'd been discussing, relieved when he took the bait. He rattled on about the protagonist, forgetting the spice jars entirely.

The problem was, once he got started detailing the plot of the last episode he'd watched, he didn't seem interested in talking about anything else. He didn't bring up work once while they cleaned up, which was the one thing she'd hoped they could discuss.

I'll bring it up over dessert. Before curiosity burns a hole in my brain.

"So, what did you find out about our Ms. Carmel?" Annie asked while enjoying a bowl of ice cream sitting on the floor in front of the fireplace. She'd gambled on flavors while shopping and picked up both cookie dough and butter pecan, unsure of his tastes. He'd surprised her by asking for a scoop of each. Annie decided to do the same, and the combination of flavors turned out to be just right.

"Not much," Adam answered. "I've tried retracing her movements since she landed in Turtle Bay a couple of months ago, but there's nothing really uncommon about the woman." He took another big bite of his ice cream and leaned toward the fire. The glow lit up his features softly in the dim light.

Annie frowned. She hadn't realized Ms. Carmel was on the Sheriff's department's radar for that long, before she'd called up Annie, her boss, and the mayor. "And where did she live before she moved here?" she asked.

"In Mexico, I think. But she's American by birth," Adam said, tilting his bowl back to drink the remnants of his ice cream. She watched him swallow, lost in thought about what all this could mean. The puzzle was assembling in her mind, though she had yet to snap the pieces together.

Adam, of course, noticed her expression and reached over to pat her hand reassuringly. "I know it's strange, but don't worry too much about it, little witch," he said calmly. "You and I can figure it out before anything escalates. We always do, don't we?"

He looked at her expectantly, and she couldn't help but smile at his confidence. She did prefer to see the good in people, but sometimes her hunches clouded her vision of the big picture. Adam was great at pulling her back to reality.

"Yeah, we do," she conceded, bumping her shoulder into his. They sat together for another hour after that, talking about everything from the weather to their case. While Adam spoke, Annie thought about how grateful she was for his friendship. After her tense divorce, she needed a reminder that men could be kind and trustworthy.

It was getting late when he finally got up off her floor and decided it was time that he head home for the night.

"Thanks for dinner, Annie," he said warmly, giving her one of his genuine, toothy smiles.

She sighed and replied, "Anytime, Adam," thinking wistfully that the night was over too soon for her liking. They could have talked all night, she supposed, and still found things to discuss.

"It's my turn to buy dinner next week. You cooked the last two weeks in a row," he said as he shrugged into his jacket.

She conceded this point and told him she wanted him to surprise her. She followed him out onto her porch to see him off, and he lingered for a moment, his face earnest in the glow of her porchlight.

"You're keeping all the doors and windows locked at night, right?" he asked, peering at her in the semi-darkness with more than a hint of concern in his voice.

"Yes, I've been double-checking since I got that call," she confessed, and a frown puckered his forehead.

"Do you feel safe here alone?" he asked in his serious cop voice. She didn't answer right away. She wasn't alone technically. She had Monty. Though, admittedly, he wouldn't be much help if she ever needed any.

"I feel safe," she said finally and knew it to be true. This wasn't Boston. What harm could possibly befall her in such a small town? Even if someone had messed with her supplies, all that had done was give her weird visions.

He took his hands out of his pockets to rest them on her shoulders. She caught her breath as he tilted his head and looked at her analytically for a moment.

"Okay then," he decided finally, giving her shoulders a gentle squeeze. "But I keep my phone right beside my bed. I know you're a big girl, but if anything goes bump in the night, please call me. Even if it seems silly. I won't mind."

Annie felt a swell of emotion in her throat. It had been a long time since anyone was concerned for her safety like this. She decided to give him another hug before he left, and he gladly accepted it. He smelled good, and he felt solid in her arms. Maybe she could be forgiven for lingering as long as she did; so comforting was his embrace.

Adam pulled away first and hopped down the three steps to the sidewalk. "Stay safe, little witch," he said from the pavement, giving her a jaunty salute.

She threw her head back and really laughed at this, thinking how good it felt to have things to laugh about. He waved before sliding into the front seat of his car. This time, she returned his favor and watched him drive away, craning her neck to watch him go, not going in until he was entirely out of sight.

Behind her, Monty manifested again. For once, he didn't offer up his opinion as the Sheriff's car drove out of sight. If anything, the apparition seemed concerned for her. He reached out a hand to place on her shoulder as if trying to offer her comfort too, which might have been nice, had Annie been able to feel him there at all.

CHAPTER FOUR

ANNIE HAD a lot to think about after Sheriff Parker left that night. Her mind immediately went to the problem at hand: Adeline Carmel had something to hide. What was even more worrying, whatever her plan was, she would likely execute it during the grand opening of her flower shop.

Her boss' comments about the mayor still troubled Annie more than she cared to admit. Could this seemingly innocent woman have a murderous plot just below the surface? And what did it have to do with Annie and her practice as a witch? She looked over at her drying rose petals and wondered how long it would be before she could use them again in her potions. More and more, she was feeling naked, powerless, even though she knew she had ingredients enough to cast many spells already. But she didn't have a fully stocked larder.

Thinking of flowers, Annie's mind returned to her own personal issue – her visions. Could they have resulted from a hallucinogen? Annie shrugged the idea away from her mind. There's no way to test for them at this stage. By now, her body would have expelled whatever she'd been given.

"Monty?" she asked as they went back into the house. "Has anyone been in the house lately besides us?"

The ghost shrugged, which raised several questions in Annie's mind. When he disappeared, where exactly did Monty go? She'd always imagined him hiding somewhere in the walls or something, but maybe he just wasn't 'there' so much as 'elsewhere'. On a spiritual plane maybe.

"You're not much help," she complained, heading back toward the kitchen, her mind already turning over other possibilities for action. There was still something she could try to help find some answers.

She knew that she would only find the answer to her dilemma if she asked her subconscious for help. To that end, she decided to prepare a revealing potion, which she would drink before going to bed. In the morning, she hoped to have the answers she needed. In truth, she wasn't even sure it would work. But she felt like she had to give every option a fair shake in this ever-growing mystery concerning Ms. Carmel.

It didn't take long to brew up the potion with all the new ingredients at her disposal. She thought over the exact words she wanted to say, knowing her intent mattered almost as much as the ingredients she used for this type of work. She scribbled a few different phrases in her notebook before she landed on a short sentence that wouldn't be hard to remember. Incidentally, it sounded like a poem, making it easy to memorize.

Warmth of liquid, consumed by night,
reveal your answer in tomorrow's light.

Warmth of liquid, consumed by night,
reveal your answer in tomorrow's light.

Warmth of liquid, consumed by night,
reveal your answer in tomorrow's light.

Annie wrote the incantation three times, then said it aloud to herself three times before drinking her home-brewed potion in one large gulp. She repeated the chant three more times while it settled in her stomach and breathed deeply, waiting for a moment in the stillness before she got ready for bed.

Monty frowned. She found that he wasn't entirely approving of her spellcasting sometimes. He made a point of sitting down in the kitchen after she'd checked the locks, signing to her that he would stand watch for the night. She was grateful for the gesture, more than she let on. Knowing he would watch over her would give her added confidence that she might truly concentrate on what the potion was revealing to her, without worrying about outside threats.

After brushing her teeth, and donning a nightgown, Annie slid into bed and turned off her light. The potion was already working, for she could feel the growing heaviness in her limbs. She had only moments before it would become impossible to keep her eyes open. Already, she was heavy-lidded and lethargic.

I will have all the answers I need when I wake.

Satisfied she'd done all she could, she pinned her hopes for the morning on her skills in potion-making and drifted off to sleep, tucked up tight under a homemade quilt for extra protection. Adam's concerned eyes flashed into her mind as she dozed off. Her friend cared about her. It was a lovely thought to hold close in these final moments of wakefulness.

The next morning, Annie woke up with the sun, groaning at its brightness streaming through her window right into her eyes. She thanked the powers that be that it was finally Saturday. Not that Annie could really rest, of course. At two o'clock, she would be attending Ms. Carmel's grand opening. Her stomach churned at the thought, but her mind was alight with curiosity. She hoped her hunch was wrong, and that this whole thing was nothing more than a big misunderstanding.

She knew that wasn't likely.

Her night had been relatively calm, much to Annie's disappointment. The potion she drank the previous evening had left some effect on her awareness, but the answers she sought were still not very clear.

She threw back her blankets and padded over to her bathroom, donning a fluffy robe and some fuzzy socks to fight off the morning chill. She looked at her reflection and shrugged. This was as good as Saturday morning was going to get under the circumstances.

She made her way to the kitchen and went to the pantry to get some fresh eggs to prepare her favorite weekend breakfast – French Toast. As she was gathering ingredients, Annie noticed a box of truffles lying out in plain sight on the top shelf.

What is that doing here?

Since she had cleaned the pantry thoroughly two days ago, she was relatively sure there had been no truffles there before.

"Monty? Did you see something last night?"

It occurred to her she hadn't seen the ghost since she'd woken up. Bored with guard duty and back to the ether? Or something else entirely?

She didn't like the uneasy feeling these thoughts gave her. Thoughtfully, she took down the box and opened it. Each truffle was wrapped in that same purple gauze that now decorated Ms. Carmel's shop window. Annie felt a chill. *Something wasn't right. Could the truffles be poisoned?* Gingerly, she brought her nose closer to the box and recoiled immediately at the smell. The aroma was subtle and likely would have gone unnoticed if she hadn't been looking for it.

She grabbed a book from her shelf, thumbed through it looking for the exact page, and read it a few times to be sure. She had her answer, but it certainly didn't clear up her conundrum with Ms. Carmel. *I think I know what you've put in these truffles, Ms. Carmel,* Annie thought to herself. *But why is my question? And how?*

And where is Monty?

Annie hovered by the garbage and hesitated to throw the box out. Her gut told her to keep it for the time being and she replaced the box on the top shelf and closed the pantry door. She was unsettled, but she tried to go about her routine. The toast she made wasn't as crisp as usual because she was distracted and took it out of the pan too early. She also forgot to get more syrup at the store yesterday, so her breakfast was drier than she preferred. But she soldiered on, made herself a nice pile of French Toast using honey, for a change, to make it sweet, before she sliced up a grapefruit to go with it. Thoughtfully, she set her kettle on the stove for tea.

Still troubled, Annie had a leisurely breakfast and a nice cup of tea while she read the Turtle Bay Gazette. What she was looking for exactly, she didn't know. She scanned the few pages of the weekend edition in seemingly no time at all. There wasn't an article about the shop opening, to her surprise. Still, there was a nice piece about a local girl whose charity toy drive was so overflowing with donations that she could give some to a nearby town as well. Annie smiled. For she had seen the donation table set up in the village square and had added a little charm to the display, which was guaranteed to make people feel a little more generous.

Annie spent some time doing the crosswords and then decided to make some headway with her cleaning. She dusted the fireplace and her kitchen shelves. She even swept her hardwood floors and vacuumed her living room rug. Monty didn't return, even though this kind of frenetic activity tended to draw him out. In her experience, most ghosts were curious about what the living did and tended to gravitate toward activity.

With this in mind, Annie made her bed, started a load of laundry, wiped down her kitchen counters, and cleaned her bathroom mirror before she let herself take a break. Any other weekend, this type of domesticity would be grounding. This weekend, chores were more of a distraction than anything, especially since Monty still hadn't appeared by the time she was done.

The clock told her it was twelve-thirty. Frowning now, she decided to get ready for the opening to distract herself from the mysteries that seemed to be piling up around her. With Monty missing and the laced truffles sitting in the pantry, she was amazed that she could concentrate on anything at all.

Firmly, she told herself it would be better to be prepared early than to arrive late to a potential crime scene, and she forced herself into the bedroom to lay out her wardrobe for the day.

Her outfit of choice for the opening was a bit nicer than the one she'd thrown on to go shopping. She picked a simple cream turtleneck sweater, some tight black pants, and loafers. She wanted to look presentable but still move quickly if the situation called for it. Annie pinned her hair up in a sleek braid and donned some evil eye earrings in case she needed to ward off someone's ill intentions. The necklace she put around her neck had a raw amethyst dangling off the end, another measure of psychic protection. Annie frowned as she fingered the amethyst. She couldn't remember the last time she was so concerned about her outfit. She secretly hoped she wasn't being obvious in her paranoia, thankful that the setting for the crystal looked attractive on her.

At one o'clock, Adam phoned to see if she was ready to go to Ms. Carmel's grand opening. Annie answered on the first ring while applying some light makeup, cradling the phone on her shoulder while she talked. She wasn't doing much: just some concealer, powder, and mascara. But she had to admit, she did look cute dolled up a little.

"Sure am," she replied cheerfully as she put her phone on speaker mode so she could finish applying her mascara while talking to him. "And I think I'll bring her back the present she left in my house."

Adam's voice raised in pitch instantly over the line. "Do you mean to tell me the woman came to see you? And you didn't call me?"

Annie laughed nervously, "No, she didn't. But she visited me somehow in my absence I'm sure." Adam was silent for a moment, and Annie worried her confession might have upset him. She bit her lip. Thinking back, she probably should have called him the minute she found the truffles.

"What did she leave you?" he asked, and she could hear him rummaging through his closet, likely getting dressed as she was just now. "A box of truffles," Annie told him, and there was another pause while she allowed him to think it over.

"Please tell me you didn't eat any of them," he said earnestly, and she shook her head even though he couldn't see her. "No, of course not," she responded with a chuckle. "And I'm not sure why Ms. Carmel thinks I would just eat truffles I didn't buy. But I hope we find out today."

"Food seems like a risky present to leave for someone who lives alone to find," he said, thinking hard. "If you had other people buying food for you, I could see how the truffles might slip in unnoticed. But if you're the only person buying what you eat, food would not be the ominous gift I would choose to leave you."

"I agree," Annie said, "but this is the same woman who lied to multiple people about how she got their personal contact information. We may not be tracking a career criminal here. It seems kind of desperate."

Adam hummed on the other end, considering her words. "Astute observation, little witch," he said, and she could hear the smile in his voice. "She does seem to want your attention very, very badly. We just need to know why before she does something worse than leave you candy."

Annie agreed, and they settled on a time to meet up at the shop. Adam hung up, and she finished her makeup with a swipe of nude lipstick and smiled at herself in the mirror. Today was going to be interesting, to say the least. She couldn't *wait* to find out why this woman was so obsessed with her and why she was lying and sneaking around. She only hoped they wouldn't be too late, and that no harm would come to any innocent parties because of Ms. Carmel.

Now if she only knew where that ghost went!

CHAPTER FIVE

ANNIE HAD to scrape some lingering ice off the top of her little yellow car before she could leave. A curtain moved next door, and Annie waved. She wondered if her neighbor was home, or if perhaps they had a ghost trying to catch her attention. The thought put a damper on her mood, and she glanced back at her own house uneasily before getting into her car. *Where are you, Monty?*

She cranked the heat up and drove off, eager to meet Sheriff Parker and get started on this mystery. She had a gut feeling that everything would turn out alright, and her gut feelings had never steered her wrong before. The radio was playing the news, and she listened eagerly, hoping not to hear of anything devastating happening overnight. The broadcast was, thankfully, very dull, and Annie breathed a sigh of relief to know that no new tragedies awaited her.

Adam was waiting when she pulled up and parked behind him on Garden Street. He leaned against his civilian car, wearing blue jeans, a leather jacket, and a plaid button-up underneath. *He looks very nice today*, she thought privately to herself.

His hands were tucked into his pockets, but he raised one to her in greeting when she turned off her car. As she got out, she remembered that she hadn't brought a bag today, not wanting to be weighed down.

She realized, as she walked over to him, that her outfit had no pockets. Damned women's pants. She had no place to put her keys.

"Hey," she said by way of greeting, and he nodded at her. Sheepishly, she held up her keys and asked, "Any chance you'd be willing to keep these in your pocket? I didn't bring a bag, and my outfit doesn't have any pockets."

He looked her up and down, his eyes flashing in amusement and a hint of something else. She blushed as he extended his hand to take them. She carefully placed the keys in his large palm that held the weight of her keys. Her fingertips brushed his, sending a tiny electric charge sizzling through her.

Oh my...

"I'll keep them safe for you, little witch," he said with a wink, and she laughed.

"I appreciate it. Are you ready to go in?" she asked, glancing down the street and wondering if the cars parked along the road were for the store opening or were just the usual Saturday shoppers.

"I came prepared," he said. It took her a minute to realize that he was trying to show her the inside pocket of his jacket where he had his badge tucked just in case.

Adam held out his arm to her. The sidewalk was icy, so she took it, and they made their way a few blocks down the road to Ms. Carmel's flower shop. Neither of them said anything as they walked. Still, Annie could feel how anxious Adam was just by his body language. *Most people wouldn't be able to see the tense way he's holding himself,* she thought. But after months of working closely together, she could tell when he was on high alert. She squeezed his bicep reassuringly, and he reached up to pat her hand in return. *At least I don't have to do this alone.*

When Adam and Annie arrived at the flower shop, they paused outside the store and looked through the front window before going in. From what they saw, it looked like the festivities had barely started. Some guests had arrived already, but not many. She counted fifteen people milling around. Half of them looked like they worked there.

Adam opened the door for her. Annie's senses were instantly assaulted with the overwhelming smells of all the flowers inside. She wiped her wet shoes on the mat, and Adam did the same. They both needed a moment to get used to the sights and smells that awaited them inside.

The entire shop was decorated with satin white and lilac purple draperies, dotted with elegant flower arrangements placed in a pattern around the space. She admired the design for a moment.

Adam wasn't quite so appreciative. "It looks like a wedding reception threw up in here," he whispered to her. Annie chuckled but swatted him lightly on the arm all the same.

"Behave yourself," she murmured, signaling that they should mingle. They said hello to a few people, trying hard to look as though they were nothing more than a pair of friends interested in what the new establishment had to offer.

They took a few minutes to explore the area since it hadn't gotten crowded yet. Adam didn't see anything amiss. He was silent as they made their way around the room methodically, but he stayed tucked close to Annie. She could feel the heat from him when he stood next to her, and it calmed her nerves. However, what attracted Annie's attention were the boxes of truffles inside the glass display cases. They seemed almost unnoticeable to unsuspecting guests. The boxes were tucked out of the way, but they were easy enough to spot since Annie had an identical one at home. She decided not to draw attention to them but subtly pointed them out to Adam.

"The ones I got are just like that," she said in a low voice, keeping the conversation between them. "And I'd bet anything they smell off, as though they've been doctored somehow, like mine."

Adam scrunched up his nose at that. "You sure?" he asked and moved closer as though to shield her from the truffles. "Better keep an eye on who goes back there then," he said, and she nodded in agreement.

She took his arm again. They found a spot to stand out of the way, where they could observe the space more fully, while still being close enough to overhear any conversations in the room. There was a low hum of voices, but the room was relatively peaceful at the moment. Annie took a deep breath and let her eyes scan the room again, trying to see any details she'd missed on their first walkabout. She was glad again for Adam's presence next to her. It gave her room to clear her mind without worrying about watching her back too.

That's when she saw Monty. He hovered behind the crowd, nodding toward the vases of elegant purple and white flowers that decorated the back of the store – in front of some sort of illuminated backdrop to make them look appealing. It took a second for her mind to catch up, but Annie was astounded by what she saw. She turned to Adam and pulled on his arm, nodding in the direction of the vases of flowers backlit by white lights. He looked at the flowers, then back to her with brows raised.

"Do you know what those are?" she asked, eyes wide. She struggled to keep her voice quiet. He shook his head and leaned in closer to listen to her. "The purple ones are foxgloves – highly toxic– and the white and blue are Salvia."

Adam turned his head sharply to peer into Annie's eyes and said, "You mean, as in *Salvia*, the drug?" Annie nodded emphatically and replied, "And if I'm remembering my senses correctly, I think the box of truffles she left at my place is filled with truffles laced with Salvia." Adam looked stunned by this observation, and she kept talking.

"When I had my hallucinations during our latest investigation, I had some mint tea. I think Ms. Carmel somehow dropped some Salvia in my herbal tea jar."

Adam looked even more floored by this revelation. Annie thought if she pushed him slightly, he'd fall right over.

"Why do you think she's doing this?" Adam asked, his jaw tight. He was holding himself rigid, clearly becoming angrier with each new detail she revealed.

Annie considered her answer, not wanting to worry him further, but wanting to be truthful about her theories. She rested her head on the wall behind them and chose her words carefully.

"I would not be surprised to discover that she might be a witch who learned her trade from a Mexican Shaman," she said with confidence, hesitating on the word 'witch' because it was hard to be sure. Sometimes people just dabbled, with the intent of enacting petty revenge or causing harm. Her eyes met Monty's from across the room and she saw the concern etched upon his face. He didn't even flinch when someone walked through him.

A 'bad' witch then, or Monty would not be so worried.

Not for the first time, she wished she could just talk to the ghost. It was always so difficult to communicate. She had no idea Monty could even visit other locations. Had he disappeared so he could hunt the person who had put the truffles in her house?

She shook her head. Now was not the time to get distracted. Adam looked uncertain. She could tell he believed her, but the circumstances themselves were a hard pill to swallow. He was not a witch, and Annie was the first person he'd met who openly practiced her craft and used it to help people. He didn't understand the dynamics of her world very well yet. To him, this was all unknown territory.

Of course Adam was an experienced police Sheriff. But he was at a loss in dealing with *this* sort of criminal. He was used to homicides, robberies, and plots to commit fraud or embezzlement. But attempted poisoning cases didn't usually land on his desk. Slipping some Salvia into Annie's tea would be hard to prove in court and likely wouldn't result in a conviction. Especially since she'd already destroyed anything that could have been used as evidence.

I should have been more careful perhaps…

As for the truffles being laced with a toxin, he didn't know what to make of that information. His palms were clammy. "You might have become violently ill," he said under his breath, and the look he gave her sent shivers down her spine. "Or worse."

He was right. If she hadn't been paying attention, she might have tried one of the truffles. As he was pondering, Annie squeezed his arm again, wanting to reassure him somehow, but still needing to ask the question that was preying on her mind. Monty had moved across the room now and was stalking the staff as if looking for something.

"Do you know if the mayor has a heart condition?" Annie asked unexpectedly. She hated asking out loud and whispered the words in Adam's ears.

He shivered a little at her breath on his ear, then he turned to her, eyebrows raised. Adam answered in his own whisper, "No idea. But what are you thinking?"

Annie turned Adam away from the small crowd formed around the hostess and led him into a far corner. They could be tucked away and mostly hidden from prying eyes by a large plant. He went willingly. She could see he wanted to be as close to her as possible now that he knew she had come face-to-face with a deadly poison in her own kitchen earlier today. Her stomach was still knotted-up just thinking about it. She gave him credit for keeping his composure.

"I think that she's laced the truffles she'll give to the mayor with Salvia. It's a fast, effective hallucinogen that will give him frightful images. If he's got a heart condition, extreme anxiety could trigger an attack. And if she's added digitalis from the foxgloves, the combination will be lethal. Even if you ask for an autopsy, by the time you get the poor man on the ME's table, the drug would have disappeared from his system."

CHAPTER SIX

"BUT WHY?" Adam asked, aghast. "Why would she do such a thing?"

Annie looked around her again to make sure no one was listening to their conversation. "Simply because she can, Adam," Annie explained as gently as she could. "And she's invited me here to watch her show off her powers, to make sure I understand that she's a force to be reckoned with. Bad witches are like that sometimes; thirsty for power and seeking enemies to torture at will."

Adam was dumbfounded. He scratched his head and took a moment to absorb all the information that had been thrown at him in the past few minutes, but he came up empty. "So, how do we get rid of her?" he asked. "My hands are somewhat tied. Until she makes a move on someone, which we can prove, there are no laws being broken. People are allowed to have toxic plants, or even poisons, in their homes. There has to be deliberate intent. An attempt, preferably where we can witness the action if you expect the law to deal with this.

The law. A bad witch would hardly care about the law.

"I'll have to destroy her somehow," was Annie's frightening answer. Adam looked her up and down with a critical eye this time. She was slight and short, but he didn't doubt her power as a witch. He was, however, worried about his friend going up against someone so bloodthirsty. Especially in such a cold-blooded way.

"And exactly how are you going to do that, little witch?" he asked, looking down at her and trying to observe her facial expression. Did he feel helpless since he had no magical abilities? For all she knew, he had very limited knowledge about poisons and murderous witches. Annie thought about his question, and they both watched as more and more people flooded into the room for the opening. No sign of the mayor yet, though.

"Honestly," she said after a pause, "I think our best bet is to intercept the truffles and have them tested. I mean, the only reason to poison candy is that you intend for *someone* to eat it. We don't have to prove which person was the intended victim, do we? But we need to do it without drawing too much attention."

Adam nodded in agreement and added, "We don't want to spook the mayor or Ms. Carmel. Or any of the other people here, for that matter. I don't know about you, but I don't feel like dealing with a mass panic today over a few truffles."

Annie's eyes widened at his implication, and she agreed, "We'll just have to insert ourselves into their conversation once he arrives. The mayor is nice, so I'm sure he won't mind. And I suspect that Ms. Carmel will be too single-minded to think we're onto her. Clearly, she's bold and overestimates her abilities."

This time, Adam took Annie's arm and led her back to the gathering, closer to the entrance. He released her, but she stayed close to him. Monty looked up as she passed him and seemed equally relieved to see her doing something. By now, he was circling the cases of truffles as though trying to stand guard over them.

The mayor hadn't arrived yet. This at least gave them a minute to gather themselves for whatever came next.

Adam took a deep breath and noticed Annie doing the same. "Are you okay?" he asked, genuine concern in his voice.

She didn't answer for a moment. The stark reality of her situation wasn't lost on her. She could've been poisoned today, could've never seen Adam again, and might not have survived. Nothing was certain at all. The thought almost brought tears to her eyes, but she tamped them down. Adam watched her struggle and gave her space to process without asking any more questions. He was not a stranger to companionable silences, and he wanted her to be able to breathe easy after today.

"Yeah," she answered after a long pause and looked up at him with sad eyes, "I just...can't believe I was that close to an irreversible decision."

Adam sighed, and Annie sighed. Then, they looked at each other. She allowed him to hold her eye contact, and she knew what he was trying to say. "At least we can prevent the mayor from coming to any harm," he offered by way of distraction from the intensity of their emotions. "Your house being broken into is scary, but it actually is going to solve this case for us."

Annie conceded he was right. "True! And at least she, or they, did it while no one was home. Could've been way more dangerous."

They were distracted from their conversation when the mayor walked in, followed by his small security detail and personal assistant. Annie and Adam noticed that Ms. Carmel had abandoned her little gathering to meet the mayor, as the kindly old gentlemen greeted the room with a smile. This gave Annie and Adam a good look at their hostess.

Ms. Carmel was a short, older lady with white curly hair coifed into a neat bun. She wore a black dress, a black shawl, and a black covering on her head. A single piece of jewelry accessorized her outfit: a silver snake bracelet coiled around her right wrist. She was so witchy in appearance, it was almost cliché. How no one else noticed this was beyond Annie.

"Mr. Mayor, so nice of you to come. I hope it wasn't too much of an inconvenience," Adeline Carmel said with a lilt in her voice and a sickly-sweet smile plastered on her round face. Her brown eyes sparkled in the light. Under different circumstances, Annie might've even said she was a beautiful, stately woman.

"Not at all, Ms. Carmel," Mayor Davidson answered. "Always pleased to see new businesses popping up in my city." He reached over to shake her hand, and Adeline eagerly accepted his touch. She nodded silently and turned quickly away from the mayor to take a box of truffles out of the case nearest to her and handed it to the man himself. She said, with an air of foreboding, "I think you might enjoy these."

She gave him the box of truffles triumphantly, only for her face to fall slightly when he said, "Thank you very much, Ms. Carmel. I'm sure my grandchildren will enjoy them."

Adeline was stunned. She hadn't been expecting that response. She was an experienced manipulator, though, so she rallied quickly. "Wouldn't you even taste one before I start selling them?" she asked. Her words dripped with fake sweetness.

"I'm afraid not, Ms. Carmel. My heart wouldn't appreciate it," the mayor chuckled. "But as I said, my family will love them, I'm sure."

Adam gave Annie a look and decided to intervene at that very moment. "Let me take the box for you, Sir," he offered, taking the box of truffles out of the mayor's hands, "I'll have your aide put it in the car."

Mayor Davidson smiled. "You do that, Sheriff. Thank you." He turned away from Adam and went on to admire the shop's décor while Annie laughed silently to herself. Her little suggestive power had worked. *Adeline will not be able to go very far in this town,* she mused. Adam strode back to her and slipped the truffle box into his jacket as he'd done with her keys.

"Mission accomplished," he whispered and turned to lead her to the exit. Annie stopped him first and asked him to wait. She walked over to the still-stunned Ms. Carmel and extended her own hand.

"Ms. Carmel?"

An unpleasant expression flitted across her features. "That's me," she said, in a faux-chipper tone. "Can I help you, dear?"

"I just wanted to thank you," Annie said, pointing to the truffles in the case, "for the sample box that was delivered to my house. Directly into my pantry, in fact. I had no idea you did delivery already."

Ms. Carmel straightened up, and her eyes scanned Annie for a moment before the realization hit her. "Annie Archer, I presume," is what she said, but her eyes burned with anger.

"The very same," Annie said, grinning impishly at her. She could feel Adam walk up behind her, and she reached up to poke him in the chest without breaking eye contact with Ms. Carmel. "And this is my close, *personal* friend, Sheriff Parker."

Adeline's eyes flitted up to meet Adam's. She grimaced with the realization that she'd been caught in at least one lie today.

"Nice to meet you," Adam said curtly. "Though my boss is under the assumption that you and I have spoken frequently since your arrival, Ms. Carmel."

For a moment, Ms. Carmel stared them both down. Annie could feel the power residing just under the surface of the older woman, and it nearly made her lose her nerve. But Annie knew that she was on the side of *not* murdering the mayor, so she stood her ground.

"Well," Ms. Carmel started with her hands clasped together. "Nice to meet you both as well. I do have other guests to greet if you'll excuse me." She rudely scooted around them and flew to another group of people, making her grand entrance and gracing them with her large smile and musical laugh.

She turned to Adam, and he was watching Adeline with a fire in his eyes Annie had never seen in him before. He was angry; and angry on her behalf at that. He also didn't want to leave so long as there were still truffles in the store. How many more people would Ms. Carmel target before she was done.

Unless...

She glanced over to Monty who was hovering near her. He was able to handle small objects such as the remote control at home. Maybe he could do a bit more here. "Let's get out of here, Sheriff," she said, looping her arm through his once again, "I think we have some work to do. I do believe you have my keys though. I would hate to be *locked out*..." Annie silently signaled to Monty that it was his time to shine.

Monty stared at her a long moment from under his bushy eyebrows. He gave her a stiff, polite nod the way a soldier who was accepting orders from a superior officer would. A moment later, she saw him with a set of keys, carefully moving to each case of truffles and locking each one.

Annie smiled. She had no doubt he would 'lose' the keys somewhere when he was done.

"Annie...?"

Adam couldn't see any of this, of course. He was looking at her strangely and she wondered, not for the first time, what he would think if he knew she didn't live as lonely a life as he thought she did.

One thing at a time, Annie, she cautioned herself. "Shall we go?" she asked again, and this time Adam didn't protest when she asked him to walk her to her car.

They carefully deposited the suspicious truffles into his vehicle first. He handed her the keys after fishing them from his pocket and said, "I'll get these to the lab for a tox screen. You go home and put yours somewhere safe, okay? You can bring them by the station the next time you come in, and we'll enter them as evidence."

She nodded. Adam opened her car door and made sure she was secured before he added, "I'll call you later. If anything else strange happens..." he trailed off, and Annie smiled at him.

"I will call you first thing. I promise," she said, and he looked relieved.

Annie received a copy of the lab report on the truffles' content and analysis in a few hours. How he got this information so quickly on a weekend, she had no idea. She suspected Adam might have called in a few favors somewhere. She apparently wasn't the only one with secrets.

She smiled to herself and did a little victory dance in her kitchen. Monty popped in while she was making a ruckus and shook his head when he saw her. But he was smiling, and she knew he wasn't upset.

"We're going to need to talk, you and I. I want to know how you can wander around this town. I thought ghosts haunted buildings. I didn't know they could leave."

Monty smiled. It was disconcerting if you looked too closely at him. He was fading fast and seemed pale around the edges. She wondered if the day had tired him somehow. Perhaps his actions had depleted something he was having trouble getting back.

Before he disappeared completely, she cast a charm in his direction, something she used to help someone build up strength after being ill. She had no idea what it would do for a ghost, or even if it would have any impact at all. But she was rather fond of the old man and wasn't entirely inclined to have him fade out completely on her just yet.

"Get some rest!" she shouted after him as he disappeared. She chuckled when he saluted her with a single finger, something he had picked up from watching television no doubt.

The rest of the weekend was uneventful, thankfully. She saw Adam again on Sunday, and they both shared in the joy of a case well-solved by ordering takeout and watching that show Adam had been obsessed with.

Later that night, she phoned Rosemary to tell her what had happened. Rosemary was bowled over by the revelation, not thinking a witch would try to take out a fellow witch so brazenly.

"What about the foxgloves. Do you think she's extracted the digitalis from the flowers and stashed it somewhere?" Rosemary inquired.

"I don't know. But since she's being charged with attempted murder on the person of the mayor, you can be sure her house and garden will be searched thoroughly," Annie replied. Rosemary breathed a sigh of relief, and Annie did too.

"Okay then, but I think you should change the locks around your house and get rid of the truffles before someone gets hurt," Rosemary suggested.

Annie erupted in laughter. "Wouldn't you know it? Adam had all of the locks changed on Sunday," she exclaimed, and Rosemary chuckled. "He even took the truffles to the station already. He said he didn't want them around the house another moment as if they would jump out and attack me when my back was turned."

"That Adam seems like a good guy to have around," Rosemary mused, and Annie quieted down.

"He is," she said thoughtfully, "I'm glad he's my friend."

Friend. Funny how it was getting harder to say that word. She remembered that little electric tingle when she'd touched his hand by accident.

"I'm glad too, dear," Rosemary said. "Someone's got to keep an eye on my Annie for me when I'm not there."

"Well, he was here two days in a row, so he's watching out for me," Annie said, looking out the window at the sun setting just behind her trees. Rosemary said her goodbyes and told Annie to thank Sheriff Parker for her.

As she got ready for bed that night, her phone rang again. It was nearly ten o'clock, but Annie answered it.

"Hope I didn't interrupt anything, my little witch," Adam's voice rang out over the line, and she rolled her eyes.

"Nope, just getting ready for bed, Sheriff."

He chuckled at her, and she continued through the house, turning off lights as she went, lingering in the dark, just because it felt cozier talking to him that way.

"I just called, uh, to say that I'm glad you're safe after everything that happened this week. And you know if you need me, I'm just a call away," he finished a bit sheepishly.

Annie settled down in her bed with the phone pressed to her ear. "I will. Thank you, Adam. For everything."

She didn't elaborate, and he didn't make her. They said goodnight, and she hung up the phone. Annie wouldn't need a potion to sleep tonight. Her new locks would keep out her enemies. Monty was somewhere nearby, and her friend a few streets over brought her enough comfort that she was able to drift off into a peaceful sleep, secure in her cozy, haunted home.

The End

AN ANNIE ARCHER PARANORMAL MYSTERY

THE CASE OF THE

MISSING MILLIONS

A COZY MYSTERY

DAISY LANDISH

PROLOGUE

STEVEN LANGDON PULLED on the sleeves of his sport coat and tried to exude confidence as he walked across the bar. That was what he called 'the long walk' as though this was a set path he had to take. In a sense, it was. How else would he reach the pretty girl perched on the barstool opposite the mirror, just waiting for the right guy to make the right move? He knew this for a fact, for he could see how she watched the room in her reflection.

Realistically, Steven wasn't expecting much, even if he put his best strut into play: holding his shoulders back, gut sucked in as he made this particular trek. The long walk ended with rejection more often than not. But it was better than staying home with frozen dinners and reruns. And occasionally, it yielded results.

This woman was way out of his league, even if he was sure she had winked at him. Maybe he was wrong, perhaps she had something else in mind or was looking at someone else, but if there were even a chance with her...well, he'd be a fool not to take it.

So, he strolled over with a well-practiced charming smile and stood next to where she was sitting. She'd turned to watch him approach, her back was to the bar, and her long, shapely legs were on display. She wore a short-back dress, and a necklace glittered in the neon lights surrounding the bar, glittering and expensive. Her hair cascaded down her back in waves giving her a sophisticated look at odds with her pixie face and upturned lips, which hinted at sin and mischief.

She watched him from the corner of her eye, and when she did not object to his presence, he took a chance and slung one leg over the stool next to her. If anything, she seemed to smile a bit more as he sat.

Good God in heaven. She was actually smiling right at him.

She twisted on her perch so she was looking directly at him, and her lips curled into a smoldering grin that sent electricity sparking down his spine. "You certainly took your time getting here."

He was at a loss for words. Not only had she indeed winked at him, but she'd waited for him. And he had kept her waiting. He kicked himself for that, at the same time, not believing his luck. While trying to find an appropriate response, he stalled by waving down the barkeep and he ordered another round for them both.

"I wanted to know there wasn't another rooster on the porch."

Okay, maybe not the best opening line, but his mother had always said to be himself. And this was about as real as it got. Maybe it was better in some ways to get these awkward fumbling lines out of the way right out the gate, so they could focus on getting right to the point.

She looked at him for a long moment and then burst into laughter. It was a throaty, deep laugh. He mentally kicked himself, thinking this whole game was over before it started. He made a movement to turn away, anger kindling in the pit of his belly though it was hard to say whether it was directed at her or himself.

"Wait, you." She turned further to retrieve her new drink from the bar, and her knees touched his. She seemed unaware of the contact or at least unconcerned. Or maybe…it was deliberate? She hadn't been put off, even if she'd seemed amused.

Steven drank his beer almost desperately as she made inroads into her margarita. From the glasses around the bar, he couldn't tell if it was her second or third, but if it had been more than that, she would have been showing more signs of drunkenness. Or she could really hold her liquor. He wasn't sure what he thought about that. His mother had also told him nice girls didn't drink, and so far, his mother had been right once tonight. This new detail added a hint of uneasiness. Of dislike.

Only the woman was talking, introducing herself as Carla Mendes, and offering her hand. Ladylike in accepting the pressure of his fingers against hers. Maybe his mother was wrong about some things.

He relaxed, settling into the conversation. This proved disappointing, too, for other than her name, she wasn't too forthcoming with information about herself. The conversation returned to him as if she found him fascinating when he pressed.

As she faced the bottom of the empty glass, he hesitated. She wasn't drunk, but another would likely push that over the edge. On the other hand, if he didn't buy another round, he would look cheap. He wasn't used to ladies who were this fancy.

The decision, ultimately, was taken out of his hands. "Hey," she laid a hand on his thigh and squeezed it. "I have an idea; let's continue this conversation someplace…quieter."

Steven smiled, thinking how nicely that settled things, and stroked her arm to convey just how much he liked the idea. "I like the sound of that. What did you have in mind?"

"I've got a hotel," Carla waved off the details as though they were insignificant. "How about we go back there? I might even have an extra bottle somewhere we can tap into." Her hand slid up his thigh, and Steven knew that he would agree to nearly anything this beauty would ask of him. "You drive," she added, "I'm not sure I should."

Steven jumped off the barstool, thinking that if this was the way his luck was going, he should buy lottery tickets. Carla was incredible. She could have been a model or a beauty contestant. Something. Something well out of his reach. And here she was, asking him to go to her hotel.

He settled the final bill at the bar with a shaking hand and offered his arm to Carla. She gave him a curious look and took his elbow, smiling.

The warmth rose from the tar of the parking lot, despite the cool of the evening. She grabbed his arm tighter, partially because she wasn't very steady on her high heels.

"This is your car?" She let a low whistle express her appreciation for the ride. "Nice."

Was it? He looked at his car, an ordinary grey sedan, and wondered. He kept it nice, sure, but it wasn't anything special. Though who was he to argue? Maybe this Carla liked sedans. Or Toyotas. Did it matter?

Steven palmed open the door and handed her in like a lady climbing into a carriage. The interior of his car nicely framed her long legs, and if her skirt rose slightly, she didn't seem too concerned.

He nearly sprinted over to the driver's side and slid into the car beside her. "Where to?"

"I can't remember the name," she shook her head, "but I can lead you there. Just turn right out of the parking lot and go about a mile."

She pointed to another left, another right, and two more lefts until Steven felt slightly uncomfortable. This wasn't taking him to the finer points in town as he'd expected. Downtown, on the Square, there was a rather lovely place. She seemed to be heading them out toward the highway.

"That's far from where we met."

"Yeah," she crossed her legs and seemed to settle in the seat like a cat with a bowl of cream. "I wanted to get out, and someone told me that was the best place for bars. They were right about that much." Her hand rested on his inner thigh. "I found you there, didn't I?"

There was indeed a hotel at the end of her directions. It wasn't... horrible...exactly, but it was much less expensive than he expected. She had seemed so...classy at the bar.

His face tightened. Pretty dress and fancy necklaces aside, he was starting to feel lied to. His mother had warned him about that too. Women who made themselves out to be someone they were not. Girls like that needed to be taken down a peg.

He parked the car and came around to get her door, thinking he would have to have a few choice words with her once they got inside.

CHAPTER ONE

"911, WHAT IS YOUR EMERGENCY?"

"HE'S GOING TO KILL ME!" The woman screamed into the phone. Where was she? The room felt sterile. A hotel? The morning sun broke through the curtains, and the woman shrunk back from the light. Her face was flushed as though from exertion. "HE'S GOING TO KILL ME!"

She paced in the shadows, darting glances over her shoulder as though something was behind her. No. Someone behind her. Where?

"Ma'am, who...who's going to kill..."

"He's mad! He's mad!"

The woman gave an ear-piercing howl and staggered back. The phone tumbled to the floor, the screen shattering under the heel of a boot. Everything went dark.

Annie Archer shot upright in bed, her breath coming in short gasps. She had been dreaming again. It was always a certain kind of dream which woke her like this, heart racing, unable to breathe. No. Not dreams. Visions.

You're not there. You're not her.

It took a minute. It always did. She was grounding herself, finding reality. She could feel the concern from her roommate, hovering silently across the room. Ghosts were not great on sympathy, however. For them, the worst had already happened. Her distress was more a curiosity than something to be concerned over.

She waved Monty off. Let the ghost find something else to puzzle over.

Why had her mind brought her to the same place all over again? Who the woman was or where she didn't know. Once again, it ended before whoever or whatever came through the door. Or was someone already in the room? She probed her mind for answers even as she tried to breathe slowly again. It wasn't there. That it was a "true dream" was undeniable. She'd had them long enough, often enough to tell the difference; whomever this woman was, her life was in grave danger. Or soon would be.

Annie lay back against the mattress, her pillowcase was soaked with sweat, and the sheets were hopelessly twisted around her. The light from the window filtered the darkness of her bedroom, and the reassuring sounds of sleepy birdsong and the world coming back to life faintly slipped into the room. It would soon be dawn and time to start the day.

There was no point in trying to go back to sleep. Not now. The same dream had come to her three times in three nights and demanded she do something about it. What exactly was somewhat less clear?

The lurid red numbers on the nightstand informed her that it was currently 4:48 am. She told herself she would have to be up in an hour or two anyway, and just now, she needed to refresh herself, get the image contained so it could be studied. Even her friend and occasional partner, Sheriff Adam Parker could do nothing without a clearer vision. What hotel? Was it something local or somewhere else entirely? What woman? Who was going to kill her?

She grabbed the notebook and pen beside the bed and switched on the light. She jotted down everything she could remember this time. The previous two entries focused on the woman, this time; she could look around the room, at least a little—no convenient signs stating the hotel's name. No "HELLO MY NAME IS" tag on her clothing to help there, either. But the room was neither luxurious, nor someplace that would rent by the hour. Mid-level accommodations. Her dress was nicely made but not expensive. The phone, however, was state-of-the-art brand new. Her purse... here Annie's fading images betrayed her. Something important teased at her memory, just out of reach. What was it?

It was gone. She could feel it there, stuck somewhere in the dimmest recesses of her brain, but when she probed at it, she found only a hollow, like a tongue seeking out an extracted tooth.

Nothing.

Her eyes drifted shut as she thought. It was too early to be up. She was floating, sleep teasing at the edges of her consciousness.

Only for a minute. A little more sleep before I start the day.

Her vision from before rewound. Started from the beginning. The woman. The hotel room. Wait. No. She was drifting further back to a bar. She saw someone she knew seated at another table. A woman she'd met at some function or another.

Real. These were real people, then. Somewhere nearby. Here the woman wasn't screaming. She was nursing a drink at the bar. Alone. Their eyes fastened on the mirror opposite her. No. She was watching the room behind her and looking for something without wanting to be noticed for looking until something caught her eye.

Annie strained, trying to see. Attempting to direct the vision but lucid dreaming techniques didn't work well on visions. The scene shifted. Back to the hotel room. The phone call. Everything was as it was before.

The call.

The cracked screen.

Everything is going dark.

Dark.

Her mind drifted. Slipped over into true dreaming until...

The alarm went off.

Annie's eyes shot open. One hand came up to push at her phone, trying to make the alarm stop. It kind of worked. The phone dropped on the floor next to the bed.

The phone dropping to the floor.

Annie started sweating. Triggered.

It's not real. It's not my phone. It is my phone, but the one I'm thinking of isn't. My phone isn't broken. It's fine.

Her hand shaking, Annie reached under the bed, fishing around until she found her phone, relieved to see the screen intact, the snooze alarm informing her she had seven more minutes of slumber.

She grimaced and sat up, wiping the sweat on her face with the edge of the sheet. The last thing she wanted was sleep.

"I need to call Adam." She spoke aloud, testing her voice in the empty room. The notepad next to the bed confirmed this. Three dreams. Four if you counted the fragment she had just had. Was it too early to wake him? She wasn't sure what shift he was on. He'd said he was working late, taking some nights on duty to relieve another man whose wife was in the hospital. Was last night one of those nights? If so, he'd have gotten off a couple of hours ago and was probably asleep.

He wouldn't mind. Annie flushed, thinking of the closeness which had developed between herself and the handsome Sheriff. Especially if she told him what she'd been dreaming. The short burst of the scene in the bar had told her she was seeing something real. The more she thought about it, the more she was sure she'd recognized a few faces in the crowd. These people lived in or around Turtle Bay, the town she called home. She wasn't chasing ghosts or fantasies; the woman who was screaming was as real as the rest.

It might not be too late to save her.

CHAPTER TWO

WHAT SHE NEEDED WAS A POTION.

Annie Archer was many things. Sure, she worked in security and had a good relationship with local law enforcement, to the point where she did consulting work from time to time with them. She also considered herself to be a pretty good friend. Not to mention she had a... well, a thing of some sort with Adam, which might be regarded as more than a friendship, even if they were taking things quickly. Casual. With benefits.

She was also a witch.

Of course, this was not to be confused with Halloween stories of evil witches who lived in gingerbread houses and ate children. She considered herself a pretty good witch who focused on good deeds. She liked finding ways to help those in her community through her potions. She wasn't above casting the occasional spell to ensure good weather for essential things like track and field day at the elementary school or the church picnic.

It was her witchcraft she needed to call on now if she was going to convince Adam, as Sheriff, to look into things officially. She simply needed more details than she had from her visions. She required a combination of self-hypnosis and perhaps a dab of something to enhance her memory and give her a clearer view of what had happened.

"It's perfectly safe," she informed Monty as if he cared. He didn't. He was stalking the neighbor's cat in the garden where she was picking herbs. The cat, unlike more humans, had no problem seeing the ghost and arched its back, hissing, tail exploding to three times its standard size.

She ignored them and concentrated on the ingredients she'd gathered thus far. Memory enhancer was perfectly safe as a spell. Tricky though. Too much, and you'd be remembering every single detail of your life for the next week, right down to how your shoes pinched your toes while you were shopping to the feel of the couch cushion under your hand when you'd been looking for the remote. An overload of detail was no picnic.

But neither was dying, so maybe it was worth the inconvenience if she could save some woman's life.

Satisfied she had what she needed, she headed back into the house to prepare the potion. It didn't take long and could be ingested in tea, which would help disguise the bitter taste. While she waited for it to steep, she considered calling Adam.

No. Only when she had more answers.

Finally, tea in hand, she settled somewhere quiet and prepared herself to explore the visions again. Self-hypnosis was a new idea, brought up lately by a witch she knew well and respected greatly. She'd suggested that the hypnotic state shared many similarities to the sleep state where visions were usually seen. By putting oneself into the hypnotic state, you can retain information better and have more control over directing the vision.

Annie drank her tea and sat back to wait for the potion to take effect.

I hope this works.

Adam wasn't the happiest at being woken up. Annie had been right about him working late and going to bed not long after getting home. She chastised herself for not remembering such a simple detail why he'd told her that specifically last Thursday at 8:11 pm when they'd been waiting for the popcorn to finish popping before sitting down to watch a movie.

Annie blinked. Wow, this remembering stuff was detailed.

She shook herself away from this thought and tried to bring her focus back to the conversation she was having with a groggy Adam, who seemed to be having trouble keeping up with the details she'd been giving him.

"Yes, I'm telling you, someone has been killed in the motel. Or is about to be? It was the lion-head door knockers that tipped me off. I remember seeing a lion painted on the logo. Each knocker on the room doors were brass lion's heads. It's called the Lion's Gate Motel, and it's out by the highway."

She almost rattled off the address and phone number and stopped herself only just in time. Of course, he knew where the motel was and could likely get the number for himself.

"I'd ask how you know all these details, but I understand your visions can be quite...helpful. Little witch, you are sure about these details?"

Little witch. His nickname for her usually made her smile. Today though, Annie was struggling to focus on what he was saying. Was he questioning the details? Details were all she had. Tons of them. Too many. Of course, she was sure.

He must have caught something in her silence because he quickly added, "I'm not doubting you. History has proven to me a few times now to trust your dreams or visions or whatever you call them. I'm ... well...concerned. I didn't hear anything last night, but I can check with the desk sergeant. I'll ring you to confirm if something is happening at that motel."

It was all Annie could ask for. Her frustration was more to do with what she still hadn't seen in the visions: anyone other than the victim. She'd gone back into the same images, starting this time at the bar, but her inner camera had kept focused on the woman, on how she'd smiled and flirted. The scene had shifted there to the hallway outside the hotel room. She would never have recognized the place if she hadn't seen the lion's head knockers. The rows of doors and the lackluster orange carpet looked like a million other such places. She remembered the door knockers when she'd stopped by the hotel before on another case.

She remembered a lot of things right now. She was pretty sure she knew where she'd lost her apartment keys six years ago for the place she'd had in Boston. It was a shame, sort of, that she couldn't go and check.

In the meantime, this seemed like a good time to get caught up on tedious tasks she'd been putting off, which required much thinking. The wheels of justice did not generally grind along at warp speed. With this in mind, she pulled out the files to get caught up on her bookkeeping. No time like the present for paying bills. She even considered whether this might be a good time to shop for a better auto insurance deal.

Two hours later, she was ready to go out. Even with a detail-oriented mind, sitting and staring at numbers all day was impossible. So far, Adam hadn't called back, and her boss at the security firm had been pretty adamant that he needed her to come in today though she'd tried to get out of it. Getting the morning off had been the best she could do. Looking back, she wondered if she'd given too detailed an explanation.

"I have a few more notes to put together for the Gilbert's case file, but I'll finish that work when I get back from running a couple of errands for the community center." She'd only kept herself from explaining just what those errands might be. While her boss, Murphey, might have appreciated the additional explanation, she might have triggered his curiosity more than she had already. She usually didn't give long reasons for needing time off.

This potion is going to be the end of me yet.

Thankfully, Adam called then, giving her a new distraction.

"I might have something. Can you be ready to go in ten minutes?"

"I'll be waiting by the door."

She hung up, smiling. She had been able to hear in his voice the eagerness to track down the root of what she'd been seeing. While he might complain about her visions sometimes, it was all in a teasing way. She knew he lived for these escapades, where they could work together and do some serious good for the town.

Minutes later, she was in his car on the way to the hotel.

His eyes were bright when he picked her up, giving no hint that he hadn't had more than two hours of sleep. "You were right. Something happened at Lion's Gate Motel. Don't know exactly what yet, but we'll find out when we get there, I suppose."

"Murder?"

He shook his head. "They haven't found a body. A lot of blood in the room, though. The sheets were soaked with it. But no corpse of fractions thereof. But that's only in the room. The guys are searching the grounds."

They arrived within minutes, one of the advantages of living in a small town. You were never more than a few minutes from anywhere. Police cruisers were blocking the main entrance to the motel parking lot. Adam drove on the grass to get around them. Annie was out of the car almost before it had come to a complete stop. She didn't know how long the memory-enhancing potion would last before it wore off, and she wanted to get every detail.

With her credentials and Adam backing her up, Annie could get a peek into the hotel room. He was right. There was a great deal of blood everywhere. She remembered the woman screaming in her dream, the 9-1-1 call. They'd been too late, after all, to save anyone.

But the body. Where could it be?

She didn't have long to wait. A few minutes later, an officer called Adam to come down to an abandoned tract of land next to the hotel. In what looked to be an old garden plot, officers searched the tangle of weeds. Annie followed, listening to their conversation with avid interest.

"Here, sir. We've found something. It would likely have belonged to a woman and seems recent. We'll have it for you in a moment."

One of the investigators finished taking pictures of something in the tall weeds. Annie's mouth went dry as she waited, wondering what they had. They appeared to be focused on something relatively minor.

She had her answer a minute later when they finished with the scene, and someone used a long stick to lift what they'd found free of the overgrowth. A bra dangled from the other end of the branch, bright against the dead weeds around it.

"It looks quite new," Adam remarked, coming over to examine it.

"It looks quite expensive," Annie corrected, taking note of the fine stitching and superior materials. She knew for a fact she didn't own anything near that nice, and she didn't exactly go for the cheap stuff regarding her lingerie budget. At least not since Adam had come into her life.

The officer handled the piece of lingerie gingerly before putting it into an evidence bag. "Think it belongs to the woman who made the 9-1-1 call?"

Adam shot Annie a look that she couldn't help but notice, even if the officer they were talking to didn't. She gave a micro shrug. There was no way she could know. Her visions hadn't taken her that far.

Adam took the bag from the officer and turned it over in his hands thoughtfully as he peered through the plastic at what was inside. "Thanks, Marc. Anything else?"

Marc nodded. "Just footprints over the grass, but nothing the forensic guys could identify."

No, they wouldn't. Annie could easily see that something heavy had come through the dense vegetation, but it hadn't rained in ages meaning there would be no prints of notice. There wasn't much anyone could tell from crushed plants and broken leaves.

They truly had a mystery on their hands.

They were about to go when another officer approached from the motel office. "Sheriff, we're in luck. There's a security camera in the parking lot. They caught a car coming in last night, about midnight. A light-colored sedan, Toyota. The plate says it belongs to a Steven Langdon."

CHAPTER THREE

THE TRIP back to the station seemed more sedate and quieter, though that was likely a trick of his imagination. The drive was filled with introspection and discussion, which somehow made it feel slower. Something about going out to a call gives some anticipation, never knowing what will be there waiting. Going back was almost anti-climactic.

"So, what now?" Annie seemed to share his mood.

He turned to Annie for a moment and then focused on the road again. "Now...I try to find out this mystery girl's name, where she's from, and whatever I can find. Then I need to talk to this..." he pried the name from his memory, "Steven Langdon. See why he was there. What he knows."

"From Lexington," Annie mused. "Lexington is a rather posh area. You'd think someone from there could afford a nicer hotel. I mean, he could have taken her someplace better. Anyplace would have been better than that one."

"Nice motels ask questions."

They drove for a moment in silence. "Do you think that this guy is maybe...kinky? I mean, he spends the night with a beautiful woman in a cheap dive and then gets his jollies by killing her and slicing her up?" Annie asked in a small voice. The thought of it seemed to make her slightly ill. Of course, seeing the victim in her visions would have brought it home to her. Made it personal. Adam glanced at her from the corner of his eye and saw she was desperately hoping she was wrong. The problem was that he couldn't be quite reassuring as she needed him to be. Not when he was thinking the same thing.

He shrugged. "Don't know. It's possible, been known to happen. But…" he took a breath and tried to piece together the ideas that were only half-formed in his mind, "I don't think it's that simple. I think there's more to this than just some crazy getting satisfaction off some fetish." He considered the thoughts that had been niggling at him for a moment. "There's nobody, for one thing. That's not typical, as far as I know, in extreme cases like that. I mean, there has to be a reason for the lack of a corpse."

The car turned the light, and Annie sat quietly, apparently trying to take his words into account. "But…what? Why?"

"That is the question I want to answer. The first thing I need to do is find and interview this, Steven Langdon."

The rest of the drive was silent between them. It was a companionable silence; both lost in their private musings. It was also a comfortable silence when no one felt obligated to keep the conversation going when just being with the other person was enough.

"Hey, Sheriff." The desk sergeant called by way of greeting as they came in. "You have a visitor. In your office." He thrust a thumb toward the back of the station. "Guy by the name of…" he checked a notepad on his desk, "Langdon. Steven Langdon."

Sherriff Parker exchanged glances with Annie. She shrugged. Even she hadn't seen this coming. "Ah…put him in the interrogation room. I'll be right there." The desk sergeant nodded and picked up his phone. Parker pulled Annie over to one side. "I want you to observe from outside of the room. There's a monitor in the next room; you can get a camera feed. See if you can get any…feelings." It was the wrong word, but he was still unsure what to call whatever she did.

He led her to the observation room and turned on the monitor in time to see a tall, thinnish-looking man being led into the room. Parker stopped at his desk, grabbed a clipboard and the little information he had on the missing woman, and entered the room.

"Mr. Langdon." He held out his hand, "Sheriff Adam Parker. It's a pleasure to meet you, though I have to admit I am somewhat surprised to find you here."

Langdon shook his hand. It was a firm grip but not painful, as if he had something to prove. "My pleasure, Sherriff. I heard about...well, the goings on at the hotel, and I just figured you'd have questions for me. I thought I should come in and see if I can be of any help to you."

"We appreciate that." Parker gestured for Langdon to have a seat and took the chair next to him. It was less formal and gave a clearer image to the camera in the room. "Perhaps we can start with the name of the woman."

Langdon shrugged. "Carla Mendes." Langdon's face curled like he just smelled something a little off. "I would be shocked if that was her real name, but it was the name she gave me. Carla Mendes."

"Why did you spend the night in Lion's Gate? Surely there were more...accommodating places?"

"I don't really know. She was fairly insistent that we go to her place. I might have insisted, but I honestly couldn't believe my luck in the first place; I didn't want to blow it by putting down her hotel. I think she wanted to be 'home,' as it were, and I was a cheap ride." He waved one hand in negation. "To be honest, I would have gladly taken her anywhere away from the crowds. I did offer to take her to my place, but she didn't want to go there. Then she started talking about going away for the weekend. With me. Take a vacation someplace exotic, she said."

"So, what happened after you got to the hotel?"

Langdon shifted in his seat and cleared his throat. "That's...difficult to say. You see...I fell asleep. Early. It's not the sort of thing I do, but I literally could not keep my eyes open. I don't actually know what happened; that's one of the reasons I'm here. I really...don't know."

He took a breath and let the rest out in a rush. "When I woke up, I was alone. There was a considerable amount of blood on the sheets, but...."

"But?" Parker prompted when Langdon didn't finish the thought.

"Well, I thought it was…you know…women's…troubles. I thought maybe she had become embarrassed or something. I mean, it was a lot of blood, but I didn't think it was that much. So I dressed and headed back to town as quickly as I could. I mean…I understand sometimes accidents happen, but to have just left like that…." He shuddered with the memory. "I didn't really think more about it until I heard on the news…anyway, I thought I should come and talk to you about it."

Langdon was cooperative and friendly. Other than claiming to have slept through anything that happened, he answered every question Parker threw at him, even if it meant confessing to a rater's failed assignation with a beautiful woman.

The fact was Parker didn't have enough on him to hold him, and his gut told him that Langdon wasn't his man. He ended up thanking him for coming in and then let him go. Langdon's contact information was on file; they could always get him back when needed. Parker returned to the observation room as one of the uniforms escorted Langdon out.

"So?" He propped himself on a corner of the table that held the monitor and waited for Annie to assess.

Annie slid back from the chair she was sitting on and contemplated the empty room in the monitor. "Adam…I believe him. I don't think he did anything except fall asleep. Remember, in my vision, I saw her. I mean, she was scared and panicky, but she was very much alive. I never saw him," she jabbed a thumb at the monitor, "or anyone else, for that matter, kill her. I didn't even see him at all, but from what I saw there, I don't think he did it."

"I'm inclined to agree with you." Adam set the clipboard down on the table. "That doesn't leave us much." He crossed his arms and lifted an eyebrow. "What do you make of the bra we found? Or all the blood in the room and no dead body?"

Annie thought for a moment and then met his eyes. "I think we need to visit Carla's place and see what else we can find."

It was a good idea and exactly what he'd been thinking they should do. The Sherriff broke a slow grin. "Do me a favor. Don't run for sheriff; you'd get my job."

"No promises," Annie grinned and stood. "Especially since I'm going to be fired if I don't get to work myself at some point today. I might run just to make the mortgage."

"Then we better get moving so you don't have to. Shall we go?"

Annie grinned and took his arm. The touch of her hand on his arm made him glad she'd woken him up this morning.

CHAPTER FOUR

THERE WEREN'T VERY many apartment buildings in Turtle Bay that would be considered high-class. Those were located right on the water. These gave a hint of luxury with a view, buildings of only a few stories so as not to spoil that view, identical to the landscaping. Annie had always thought the Turtle Bay Complex was pretentious and a little boring.

To her surprise, this was not where they went.

They went past and followed the road around where it curved, leading away from the water into a moderate, middle-class neighborhood. When the car stopped outside a small building with two floors and a picture window in each corner, she reassessed everything she knew about the case.

This building, dating back to the 1960s at least, boasted of only eight apartments, four up, four down. The cream-colored brick façade was in good repair though, and the interior was meticulously clean when they stepped into the front hallway.

It just wasn't the sort of place where you would expect to find anything expensive, much less a bra which cost a couple of hundred dollars, a fact Annie had discovered by looking it up on her phone when they'd been driving.

Priorities. Just because she likes expensive clothes doesn't mean anything. She might have spent money on a few signature pieces rather than have an expansive wardrobe of cheaply made things. Don't be a snob.

Figuring she was still 'noticing' too much since her potion that morning, Annie decided she needed to back off a little, at least on some details. She allowed personal bias to creep in when she needed to keep her head in the game.

She glanced at Adam, studying the mailboxes next to the door. "She's upstairs. 2-C."

Annie nodded and followed him to the staircase, where she stopped as if she'd just walked into a wall. Only nothing was in front of her, Only the stairs and a lot of air.

"What?"

Adam was watching her from a couple of steps up. It should have been easy to follow, but when she tried again, it was as if the air had grown solid and refused to let her pass. Something which set her hair on end, really didn't want her to go another step.

"Monty?" she whispered the name, looking for the only ghostly presence in her life though she knew this was ridiculous. Monty really couldn't leave her house. This was something altogether different. Something darker. Angrier. Something which didn't live on the stairs was coming down from upstairs just to greet her.

"Adam, we need to stop. There's something wrong in the building. Can you call a janitor or something to see if anything looks off?"

Adam was already shaking his head. "We can ask someone to open the door, Annie, but only if there's no answer. And once he does, it's my responsibility to go in and check the place out. Why? What's wrong?"

Annie bit her lip. It was impossible to explain. Saying some dark energy lurked on the stair seemed silly. At the same time, whatever it was had enough power to hold her back.

Maybe it's not a 'what' so much as a 'who.' Her mind rushed to grab hold of the details. Her old enemy Ambrose Hazelton might be back in town. Could he possibly set up this kind of trap? What kind of spell would solidify air and not allow a specific person not to pass?

Unless it wasn't specific or a spell. Just her own body's reluctance to go any further.

It isn't supposed to work this way. None of this is supposed to work this way.

Her silent complaint went unheard. Thankfully, whatever was holding her back also disappeared. She staggered, not expecting the sudden freedom, and had to grab the railing to steady herself.

Adam gave her a look and turned back toward the stairs.

Upstairs, the building was quiet. A faint smell of cooked onions hovered near one door. A cat meowed somewhere, sounding like it wanted to be let outside. 3-C was in the back corner on the left. When they knocked, no one answered.

"Well, that settles it," Adam said, and Annie nodded. They would have to wait for the landlord.

Thankfully, he lived just down the street.

"I own all the buildings on this side of the road. Five apartment buildings like this, tucked between residences. Nice places. I keep nice places."

"It seems that way," Annie murmured politely as the man got out a key to the place and shoved it in the lock. A moment later, they were standing just inside the doorway, taking in the enormous disaster which had left furniture overturned and belongings scattered in all directions.

It's as though a hurricane had passed through. Annie glanced toward the kitchen, seeing open cabinets, the contents rifled. A shattered glass lay on the counter.

"This doesn't look like the usual mess an untidy person might leave. It feels like someone tore through here in a hurry," she said thoughtfully.

Adam had been going from room to room clearing the place though it was apparent the apartment was empty. He jerked his head to the side, indicating she should join them. The landlord stayed behind, staring at the mess in dismay. "Do I call the cops or something?"

"I am the cops," Adam reminded him and, shaking his head, gestured for Annie to come into the room.

If anything, the mess was more pronounced here. The closet door stood open, with only a few scattered outfits still on their hangers. A safe beside the bed was open, shelves notably empty.

"I'd say the lady of the house seems to have flown the coop," Adam said, and Annie nodded.

Still unsure what had been trying to force her to stay out of the room, Annie reached out with her senses, trying to see if her intuition was trying to tell her anything. What was it she was supposed to notice?

Or are we not supposed to notice?

She felt a pull that drew her back into the living room. She drifted around the room carefully, knowing it was a crime scene and that she wasn't supposed to touch anything. At the desk, she paused.

Here.

She tugged open a drawer, then opened the next, finding nothing other than a handful of receipts.

There inside was a small, spiral-bound notebook.

"Adam, I might have found something."

Carefully she picked up the book. The first pages seemed to be nothing more than reminders. To-do lists with items crossed out. A reminder to call the dentist and make an appointment. Unsure what she was looking for she kept flipping through. A name stood out, alone on a page with a phone number.

ALEX VENTRY: PRIVATE INVESTIGATOR

A quick glance over at Adam showed he was talking to the landlord rather intently. Not wanting to wait until he was free, Annie grabbed her phone and dialed the number. A man picked up on the first ring.

"Hi, Alex. My name is Annie Archer. I'm a friend of Carla Mendes. I'm at her apartment right now, but she's not here. Any idea where she might have gone?"

Silence. For a moment, she thought he had hung up. When the man spoke again, his words were terse. "I'll be there in five," he said and hung up.

Adam gave her a sharp look from across the room. "What's that all about?"

"I'm impulsive. What else can I say?" she answered with a shrug as the landlord walked into the kitchen, his phone out to take pictures. "What's he doing?"

"Recording damage. I assume to justify keeping the deposit." Adam crossed the room to join her and flipped through the notebook, stopping on the page with the number of the detective. "This the guy you called?"

Annie grimaced. "Not that he told me anything over the phone. I wonder why Carla needed to employ an investigator?"

A tall thin man with dark hair appeared in the open doorway which led to the hallway. "Let me answer that." He came in, hand outstretched for Annie, then Adam to shake. "Alex Ventry."

Adam introduced them both, explaining who he was and that Annie was with him as a special consultant in the investigation. "We appreciate anything you can tell us."

Alex cut right to the chase. "Ms. Mendes has hired me to find the money Mr. Harrison embezzled from Ascot and Associates, an investment firm in town." Alex looked around him, his gaze lingering on the scattered debris. "But as I can see, both subjects have escaped, haven't they?"

CHAPTER FIVE

SHERIFF HARPER TOOK a moment to let the information sink in. "And what connection did she have to this Harrison?"

Alex lifted an eyebrow. "The most primitive kind. This is where they would meet at least once each week. During my investigations, I discovered that he was paying for the apartment. She had no expenses at all, really. He was what you'd call a sugar daddy."

Annie frowned. "Wait. You're telling me that Carla was having an affair with this Harrison?" It seemed apparent, but in an investigation, the "obvious" had to be stated in so many words. Assumptions could prove costly, especially if the information were later needed in a trial.

Alex nodded and threaded his thumbs through his belt loops. "Yep. But Harrison was married, so they met exclusively here, in her place." He hesitated for a moment and seemed to reach a decision. "She hadn't paid me, so she's really not my client. She can't claim confidentiality from me anymore. Between us, Sheriff, I'm convinced that Harrison's embezzlement was her idea. She might have even orchestrated the entire thing. I expect she wanted me to establish some kind of trail, a misdirection of the sort."

"Any reason for you to say that?"

"Well, nothing I can produce as evidence, but…the fact she never paid me pretty much guaranteed I'd talk now, didn't it?"

Annie wandered back into the bedroom, leaving the sheriff and the detective alone in the sitting room. Something was playing on her mind: that purse in the vision. She still didn't understand the significance of it, but it kept bothering her.

Nothing made much sense. If Carla was on the run, why bother with a 9-1-1 call? Someone running away does not want to call attention to oneself. For that matter, why involve Langdon in the process if she was on the run with this Harrison fellow? What was the point of the blood unless this Carla was trying to make everyone think she was dead? That made a strange sense; instead of following her, the police would be searching for a dead body.

She stopped short. The purse. It wasn't a purse at all. It was a small suitcase. Carla was already packed up when she made the call. It was a relief to get that memory out, but it was probably not that helpful now; the fact that Carla was on the run was well-known.

She looked around the room for some inspiration, something to trigger…something. A flash caught her eye, something partly under the dresser. She knelt on the floor and teased out a photo from under the furniture.

A Porsche. Beautiful. It flashed in her mind, nearly painful. The vision was so strong. She snatched it up and ran back to where the others were talking. She thrust the picture into the hands of the private eye. "Is this Harrison's car?"

The PI took the photo and studied it. "Yes. That's it." He looked at her as if she had lost her mind. "Why?"

"Because."

Annie refused to take the picture back. It felt…wrong. "Because if you find the car, you find Harrison." Sheriff Harper took the picture and looked closely at the image. "He's dead," Annie said flatly. She knew it as certainly as she knew her own name. That was the flash she had felt, Harrison's death.

"Excuse me," Harper said to the PI, "I should have introduced you more properly. This is Annie Archer. When I introduced her as a consultant, I might have neglected to say in what capacity. She offers…

insights and is a former consultant using these skills to benefit the Turtle Bay Police department."

"Really?" Alex gave her a reassessing look. "You're like one of those psychics?"

"No, I'm...I...."

Adam nudged her. Annie bristled a bit. That was something she had been fighting for years, that horrid label "psychic." She had some abilities, but that put her on the level with 1-900-Dial-a-Vision, and she wasn't comfortable at all with that association. On the other hand, Adam clearly had a reason for letting this man think that of her, so she bit her tongue and let it go...for now.

"Suffice it to say that if Ms. Archer says he'd dead, you can believe he's dead." He looked at the photo again. "Let's see if we can find the car."

"It's in space number 2." Annie pointed to the small parking structure next to the building. Alex looked to the Sheriff for confirmation, who only shrugged and tipped his head in that direction.

The Porsche was easy enough to spot; the black and red sleekness of the car stood out in a garage full of mid-level vehicles.

"That's his." Alex nodded. "Gorgeous car, isn't it?"

"Yeah, it is, but right now, it's evidence. I'll have to have it impounded."

"Not yet." Annie held her hand flat over the car as she walked its length. "It's not just evidence, Adam...." She reached down to the latch in front of the vehicle; the trunk was partly open. "It's a very expensive coffin." She threw the lid to the trunk upward.

"I presume this is Mr. Harrison?" She turned to Alex, who was looking a bit green.

"Yeah. That's him. Was."

Harrison had been there for hours, at least. It was all Annie could take, and she retreated to the back of the car to get some air that wasn't tainted by the smell of death.

Was that what she felt on the stairs? Was that somehow connected to the late Mr. Harrison? That didn't make sense either, not really. He would want to be found, wouldn't he? Why block them...her from discovering the body and ensuring he had a decent funeral?

Or was it something quite the opposite? Harrison's spirit is so desperate to be discovered that he hadn't wanted her to waste time in the apartment but had instead been trying to pull her to him here so he could be found.

The poor man. Embezzler or not, he certainly hadn't deserved this.

Adam called it in, coroner, impound tow, crime scene investigation. In a few minutes, the entire garage would be locked down tightly. So would the apartment. Not that it mattered, they had exhausted every clue they could get from this place. Harrison wasn't going to be testifying, but everything needed to be logged, checked, and carefully documented.

Meanwhile, Carla was out there. Somewhere. Everything they were gathering, all the evidence in the world, wasn't going to do much unless she was caught.

Annie tried to clear her mind.

It occurred to her that she was the only one who knew with certainty that Carla was still alive. Meaning Carla had to be pretty confident about now.

It also meant they still had a chance to catch her.

CHAPTER SIX

THINGS MOVED PRETTY QUICKLY from there. The forensic guys showed up to process the apartment. Annie finally made it to work, knowing full well that it would take hours for them to examine the evidence, remove the body, and finally tow the car to the impound lot as evidence. Not that she was overly productive once she got to work. Her mind was on the case as she wondered just what the evidence would show.

The following day, they had at least some answers. Mr. Harrison had been dead for twelve to fifteen hours, coinciding with the time Carla had placed her 9-1-1 call. Annie showed up at police headquarters shortly after she got the news, eager to go over the evidence with Adam and hopefully to add a little of her insight to the matter.

"So, it looks like she must have died at the same time. A partner, perhaps? Someone who took out Harrison to get the money and went after Carla as soon as they realized what she knew?"

"No," Annie said firmly. "Carla is alive and well." She picked up a photograph of the woman from the scattered pages of the police file, which lay across the desk in front of her. "I know it."

"You can tell that from her photo?" Adam asked. "I didn't know your powers could do that."

"I know it from the evidence. Think about it. She'd led you to believe she's dead from the breadcrumbs she's left for you to follow. The bra. The blood."

"It was her blood though...they typed and matched with data from her medical records."

"Menstrual cups. Don't make that face, Adam; it's a perfectly natural thing. I would suspect, though, that she collected her own blood to cover her tracks. It's easy enough to do, and there wasn't near enough blood there to account for a murder. Even the M.E. agreed on that."

Adam thought about this for a minute. "So, we were looking for a body between the blood and the bra. What you saw was her phony 9-1-1 call. She was never being attacked at all."

"No. I suspect she returned to town knowing full well the detective she'd hired was off duty for the night." She rifled through the papers and found Alex's official police statement. "According to his statement, he'd gone to sleep when he knew Harrison was home at his apartment and had gone to bed. She must have lured him to the garage on some pretense and killed him there."

"Sounds about right. What happened after that?" A middle-aged woman with dark hair and olive skin stood in the doorway. "Agent Morgan. FBI. I believe you were expecting me." She offered her ID.

Adam rose to greet her and offered her a chair at the conference table where they'd spread out everything from the police file. Annie smiled at the older woman, liking her instantly. "The rest should be fairly easy to guess. I imagine she went upstairs, changed her clothes, packed, and took off with her suitcase in tow. I expect she was rattled, never having killed a man before, hence the mess in the apartment. She was panicking probably and wanted to get as far from there, as quickly as possible."

Adam nodded. "The crime lab is going over her computer now, trying to figure out her travel plans."

"We might not need them," Annie said, picking through the photographs again and coming to rest on one taken from her desk. "That there..." she pointed to an empty cartridge box for the printer laying on the floor next to the chair. "Were there any papers taken from the apartment? Trash, maybe?"

"I get what you're looking for," Agent Morgan said with a smile and nodded toward a box that hadn't been opened yet. "In there, maybe?"

Adam pulled the lid off the box. The notebook they'd gotten Alex's information from was on top. Underneath were some crumpled papers. "This what you're looking for?" He pulled out a poorly printed sheet, with streaks throughout the document indicating the ink had run out halfway through the job. What remained was barely legible.

"Is that a rental agreement of some kind?" Agent Morgan asked with interest.

"Charter for a boat," Annie said with sudden insight. "Destination Paris."

"A private charter yacht?" Adam asked, immediately grabbing for his phone. "I'll get someone on it. Maybe the coast guard can catch up before they hit international waters."

"Or we can extradite from whatever ports the boat shows up on the way." Agent Morgan had her phone out as well. "We'll have to get some other government agencies in on this."

Hours later, the yacht was finally spotted off the coast of Aruba. "She can catch a direct flight from there to France," Annie said when they told her.

"Already on it. We're working with the local authorities both there and in France. They'll catch her, and she'll be arrested if she's got the money with her."

It didn't sound right. Annie paced around her house after she hung up, wondering what they were missing. Monty watched her in concern and mimicked sleeping as if telling her to try going to bed to see if she could get further insight from her dreams.

Only Annie didn't need to sleep to see things. She'd had visions before while waking, and she still had some of the potion left, which would give her that fine attention to detail. The aftereffects had annoyed her for hours after the last time she'd tried it, but wasn't it worth it in the end?

She called Adam and asked him to come over.

"Normally, I wouldn't try this with someone else in the room," she explained when she got there, "but I'm afraid I might see something which is time-sensitive, and I need you to be able to act quickly if that happens."

"You're sure it's safe?" Adam asked, touching her hand lightly with his own, his eyes full of affection and no small amount of concern.

"It's safe," she assured him with a kiss and settled herself quietly in the chair she's used before. With a reassuring smile for Adam, she took the potion and opened herself to the vision again the way she had last time. She wondered if she would just see the same scenes again, the hotel room or even the bar. Instead, she saw the yacht floating in the darkness just offshore from what looked like a busy port. A woman stood at the rail watching the approaching lights from police cruisers. Frantic, she raced to the opposite rail, her eyes on another yacht anchored not far away. It was clear to see she was going to jump.

Annie jolted herself out of the vision. "Adam, she's still on board the boat. I think she's going to jump overboard. I can see her swimming...I think she's too far from the beach. There was another boat." She gave as many details as she could remember. Thankfully with the help of the potion, this was quite a lot. She even captured part of the boat's name and several letters painted on the stern.

"I'm on it."

She waited with him while he made the call. When he was done, he sat beside her, sliding an arm around her shoulders. Annie was shaking.

"It'll be okay."

"I'm not so sure. The money...what if it's lost?"

"Did you see it in the vision?"

She shook her head. Carla's hands had been empty. "By now, it's probably in an offshore account." Her tone was mournful. Had they come so far only to end up with nothing at all?

Two days later, Carla Mendes, alias Angela Regent was brought back to America to face charges of murder, fraud, embezzlement, and many others. It seemed this wasn't her first time using a man to embezzle funds from a company. It was the first time she'd been forced to kill to get away.

While it was gratifying to see the end of the case and know she'd done something important in helping to solve it, Annie couldn't help but feel like she could have done something more. She'd been warned about what Carla would do several times that night. It had simply taken her too long to figure out what she was seeing. Could she have prevented a death if she'd only acted sooner? Or had she been shown what was set in stone, what was fated to happen?

The philosophical and even moral issues of all this troubled her. She wanted to know why she was shown these visions at all. Everything had been changing so rapidly in the past year. Why was this happening to her?

She tucked these worries away and told herself she needed to move on. After all, she and Adam had done considerable good with what she'd seen. With the capture of Carla, or Angela, they had locked away a dangerous woman.

As for her visions...well, maybe she'd be given a chance to do better in her next adventure.

The End

THE CASE OF THE

MISSING COFFIN

A COZY MYSTERY

DAISY LANDISH

CHAPTER ONE

IT WASN'T OFTEN that Annie wished there were more ghosts in attendance. Even for a witch, there was something a little unnerving about spirits hanging around when they should be moving on. Not that Annie knew precisely where they 'moved on' to. She had heard several theories over the years. It wasn't just non-witches that lacked insight into the afterlife.

Today, though, she kept scanning the gathered mourners, searching for any sign that the deceased's spirit lingered.

It would be a comfort to her family, Annie thought.

A shiver ran down her spine. Even though she had gotten involved in several murder cases since she moved to this small town, this was the worst. Her heart ached for Isabella Turner, the young shining star on her way to becoming a world-famous pianist.

Now she was in a closed casket.

Annie scanned the crowd one last time. No spirits, but she spied her friend, Detective Adam Parker. Adam caught her eye, and Annie flushed. She spun her face back, hoping he hadn't thought she was looking for him.

Only a few minutes later, Adam was next to her. He touched her wrist, and when she glanced at him, she found he was frowning with a soft look in his eyes.

"Are you okay?" he asked in a whisper.

Annie nodded. "We can talk later."

Adam nodded once. He remained where he was next to her, his fingers brushing against her wrist. On a frosty morning, the warmth of his touch made her relax a little. She turned her attention back to the minister as he finished his sermon. As Isabella was lowered to the ground, a single sob broke the solemn air.

A flicker caught Annie's eye, but when she turned her head, hoping to see Isabella's spirit, the movement was gone.

Shortly after, the family moved back toward their cars. Annie and Adam hung back, waiting for the rest of the mourners to follow them before they took up the end of the line. As they made their way toward the parking lot, Annie's heart was heavy.

"Are you okay?" Adam asked again.

Annie sighed. "Yes. I just wish I had found her, you know? I couldn't get a single vision in all the potions and spells I used. I talked to my mentor, Rosemary. She has no idea why I even started having the visions, let alone why they stopped."

Her arms tightened around herself. She hated feeling as somber as she did at this moment. Usually, she was lighthearted even in the face of hardship. She hadn't felt this way since her divorce.

Adam nodded slowly. "I understand what you mean."

Annie reached for his hand this time. Her heart ached not only for Isabella's family but also for Adam. He was the one who had found Isabella.... Only too late. He'd tracked down her abductor, Jonathan Swift, and found Isabella dead.

"If I had been half an hour earlier, she might have had a chance," Adam whispered.

"And if I had been able to tap into those visions, I could have helped you find her half an hour earlier," Annie said miserably.

Adam came to a stop. They turned to each other, and Annie's breath caught in her throat. She had never seen the detective look at her this way before. His eyes smoldered, but she couldn't tell what emotion he was feeling.

"It's not your fault," he said. "And it's not my fault, as hard as it is for us to accept that. The fault lies with Jonathan Swift, and he will get his punishment for this crime."

"Want to come to my house?" Annie asked impulsively. "I baked some dinner for the Turner family and delivered it."

She didn't add that she was going to bake a spell to help comfort them in their grief. Despite the popular notion of witches, Annie considered herself a 'good witch.' Honestly, she felt the vast majority of witches were good, but there were some bad ones out there. Just a few months ago, one such wicked witch attempted to murder the town's mayor.

Most witches kept to themselves and tried not to use their magic very often. However, Annie had decided at a young age that she wanted to help people. Using her special talents was the best way she could see to do that.

Adam ran a hand through his hair. "I would like that. I don't like the idea of returning to the office; my home is just so empty. And maybe I could have one of your special teas, too."

Was he asking for a spell? Annie was surprised to hear that. Adam rarely liked to meddle with the supernatural. He'd accept her visions as help in his cases, but that was about it.

"Want to take my car?" Annie asked, arching a brow at him.

Adam nodded. "I can come back later to get mine."

Annie changed her direction slightly, heading for the bubble-gum pink Volkswagen beetle at the far end of the parking lot. As they walked, Annie glanced around the cemetery before she sighed.

"Who are you looking for?"

"I… was hoping to see something I could use to comfort the family," Annie hedged. "From everything I have heard, Isabella was a beautiful woman with a kind and generous heart to match. I can't imagine the pain they are going through right now."

Adam's gaze darkened.

"Sorry," Annie whispered.

They continued in silence. Isabella Turner had been much loved in the community before she was abducted. It was easy to see why Jonathan Swift had targeted her. It just made Annie sick to her stom-

ach, thinking that the man had been so obsessed with finding the reincarnation of his late wife that he targeted young women born the day
she died.

Even though the trial was still ongoing, everyone was sure
Jonathon would face the full punishment he could for murder. The
transcripts Annie saw of the interrogation were blood-chilling. It was
clear from how he spoke that Isabella wasn't his first victim.

He had abducted women before and, upon discovering that they
weren't the reincarnation of his wife, he killed them, calling them
'imposters' as though any of them had claimed to be whom he was
looking for.

Once they were at her car, Adam stopped with a distracted look on
his face.

"Adam?"

He jumped. "Oh. Sorry. Just thinking."

Annie took his hand in hers, concerned. He wasn't acting like
himself, either. "Tell me."

Adam stared at her for a long moment, a look of shock on his face.
Annie wasn't sure why, but she tightened her hold on him. She kept
focused on his eyes, watching as he turned over his thoughts in his
mind.

Eventually, he ran his hand through his hair again. "The last time I
interviewed him, Swift showed there were five other women he killed,
but I haven't gotten their names. I can't help but keep thinking that I
need to find them. As heartbreaking as it is for the families, they
deserve to know what happened to their daughters."

Annie swallowed hard. She wanted so badly to volunteer her help,
but the visions she had grown used to had halted. Her mentor once
suggested that she had been drugged, which was why the visions
started in the first place.

Was there a way to trigger them again?

"That's why I came here," Adam said. He slid into the passenger's
seat of the beetle.

Annie quickly rounded the car and got into the driver's side. She
turned it on; it purred to life, instantly pouring hot air. She sighed in
relief as she held her icy fingers in front of the flow. The spell she had

developed to work on cars to make them run more efficiently had worked.

"You think someone here had something to do with Jonathan Swift?" she asked.

Adam shook his head. "Not directly. I hope something will come up; maybe they will think of something. Most people don't realize how important even small clues are. Anything will help."

Annie pulled out of the parking stall and took up a spot at the end of the line. The cars were moving slowly away from the cemetery.

"I might have a way to help," she offered hesitantly.

"Are you having visions again?"

"No. But I could put together an importance spell... it might help the family remember any important details they have missed or blocked out. Or I could try a seance and contact the dead women." Her voice betrayed how much she doubted that would help.

Adam shook his head. "If I find nothing soon, I might turn to your magic. Right now, though, I hope Swift gives up the locations he buried them voluntarily."

Annie nodded once as they got to the turnoff onto the road. While most of the cars turned left, she took the right turn. "Of course. I guess I could give him a truth potion, too. I just have this awful feeling that something's not quite adding up, Adam. And I don't know why."

"Me, too," Adam's expression grew troubled, and he turned his face out the window. "Maybe it's the weather."

"Maybe," Annie agreed.

But she knew it wasn't.

CHAPTER TWO

ADAM AND ANNIE drove quietly to her house on the outskirts of town. It was a small cottage with a small yard. Annie had been planning to start a window box herb garden for some time, but life always seemed too busy for her.

Her ghostly roommate, Monty, paced around the front hall, his hands clasped behind his back when Annie unlocked the door. He looked up, and the pale, almost translucent expression turned from worry to relief. Annie gave him a reassuring smile.

Where have you been? He signed. The gash across his neck made it impossible for him to communicate any other way.

It had been a long, painstaking process for both of them to learn ASL, but at least they could have some sort of conversation now.

Adam entered the cottage behind Annie; his head bowed as though deep in thought. Upon seeing him, Monty scowled and narrowed his eyes at Annie. *You were with him?*

Annie sighed. She knew better than to think Monty was jealous, but since they had been able to talk to each other, he had become rather possessive of her time. "Let's go to the kitchen," she said aloud, "the funeral was rather draining."

Monty's scowl deepened. His form flitted out of vision, but when

Annie led Adam into the kitchen, he was waiting for them. The dead rarely seemed to be too interested in the goings-on of the living; if anything, they were curious or annoyed at the interruptions. Annie wondered if Monty had witnessed his funeral.

"Do you know who the other women Jonathan Swift killed are?" Annie asked as she went to start the kettle.

Adam slumped into a chair near the table. "There are a few possibilities, but without finding them or Swift telling us who they were, there's no actual way of knowing."

"Maybe if we found a connection between any of them and Isabella, we'd have a chance," Annie mused. She prepared the teapot with a spell-infused lavender tea. It would help them relax and hopefully clear away the cobwebs from their minds.

Adam ran a hand through his hair. "I have seen nothing. Maybe you could look through their files and see if I missed something."

"If nothing else, I'd see what they looked like. It might help with the dreams."

Adam nodded once.

The kettle started whistling, and Annie took it off the heat. "I really hoped that her spirit would be at the funeral. I can't imagine how much the family is going through."

Monty rolled his eyes as he walked back and forth, passing through Adam repeatedly.

It's like living with a cat, Annie thought.

"Her spirit?" Adam frowned at her as she poured out the tea. "Wait, were you serious about the seance?"

Monty looked alarmed. *Not in my house, you don't!*

Annie ignored Monty instead of answering Adam. "I thought about it. She might give us more information. Like if Swift was working with someone else."

"There's no evidence to show he was."

"Then perhaps if I could contact his actual wife, I could get him to—"

Adam held up a hand to stop her. His eyes were slightly narrowed, and his lips pressed into a thin line. "For starters, you aren't going anywhere near that man. I know you can take care of yourself in most circumstances, but I don't want him to so much as look at you."

Annie set the tea in front of him, startled at this display of protectiveness. She opened her mouth to ask about it but quickly shut it again. His protectiveness wasn't because of the spark between them... was it?

"All right, but I could give you information to share with him to make him spill his guts," she said, fighting to keep her cool.

"Annie... No seances. I don't believe in all that crap. Spirits, ghosts, what have you." Adam wrapped his hands around the mug of tea and stared into it with a stern expression.

Monty, who was now standing behind Adam, looked affronted. His mouth and hands both moved rapidly as though he was trying to shout at Adam. Of course, Adam had no idea that Monty was even there.

"So you believe in my magic but not in ghosts?" Annie asked carefully. He believed in her magic, didn't he?

"Of course, I believe in *your* magic, Little Witch," Adam said. He offered her a smile, but it didn't reach his eyes. "But all this other stuff? I have to draw a line somewhere."

Annie sipped her tea. The floral flavor filled her mouth as the spell started working at once, relaxing her tense muscles. She shook her head. "Then I guess if I were to tell you I have a ghost for a roommate, and he's standing right behind you, you wouldn't believe me?"

Adam straightened. He turned, and Monty gestured rudely at him. When Adam turned back, though, he was frowning. "Don't make fun of me. I can't take it today."

"I'm not making fun of you. But ghosts are real, and I have a ghost roommate."

Adam turned the mug around in his hands. "Are you safe here?"

Monty threw his hands into the air and disappeared.

"Of course. Most ghosts want to be left alone," Annie assured him. "Although Monty seems to be pretty disgusted with you right now."

Adam turned again. "I'm sorry for offending you."

Annie couldn't help but laugh. "Oh, so you believe me?"

"I will not call you a liar. But, still, I wouldn't say I like the idea of a seance or anything that will put you in contact with Swift's wife. He could decide that means you're her reincarnation."

"I'm too old to be her reincarnation."

"Annie, the man's delusional. I don't care if he's in prison; there's still a slight chance that he could get out again one way or another. And if he thinks you're connected to his wife…." Adam took a large swallow of the tea. He winced as the hot liquid seared down his throat.

Annie nodded once. "Okay. I won't. So, what do we do now?"

"The Turner family is hosting a wake tonight. We could see if we can find out any information. If that doesn't work, then your baked spells." Adam's expression changed briefly, as though he wanted to add something, but he only drank more tea.

"Adam…" Annie hesitated.

Adam looked at her curiously, and a strange longing swept through her. She wanted nothing more than to help him figure this out. She reached across the table to take his hand. "We'll find them. I know we will."

"Thank you," Adam whispered. "You don't know how much that means to me."

He squeezed her fingers, the warmth of the tea lingering on his palm. Annie's heart skipped a beat, but Monty appeared behind Adam before she could repeat anything. He pointed at the doorway, scowling.

"Come on," Annie said as she stood. "We should get to the wake."

Adam nodded, looking like he would rather be anywhere else. Annie had to wonder why this case was hitting him so much harder than the ones they had worked on in the past. She didn't want to pry, though, at least not until they had found the missing women.

The wake was being held in the reception hall at the nicest hotel in town. Everything was curtained in a somber black, and at the front of the room was a memorial display of Isabella.

As Annie and Adam entered, she spotted someone lingering near the display. They were dressed in a long black coat, and from behind, she couldn't tell what gender they were. The person's head was bowed, one hand reaching out to touch the nearest picture of Isabella. They turned slightly, looking at Isabella's parents, then abruptly spun on their heels. They disappeared through a side door.

That was suspicious, Annie thought.

But the Turners were approaching her and Adam now. She pulled her mind from the figure, promising to tell Adam about it when they had the chance.

"Mr. and Mrs. Turner," Adam greeted them with a polite nod when they stopped in front of him. "I came to pay my respects."

Mrs. Turner pulled him into a hug. "Thank you, Detective."

Adam patted the woman's back. "I... I don't feel like I deserve your thanks."

"You do," Mr. Turner said. "If it weren't for you, we never would have gotten her back. She has a proper burial now, and I hope she's found peace."

Annie stepped forward now. "Mr. Turner, Mrs. Turner. My name is Annie. I sometimes help Detective Parker with his cases. I am very sorry for your loss. Even though I didn't know her personally, I felt the positive impact she had on the community."

The Turners both gave her watery smiles. Mr. Turner pulled Adam aside, murmuring he wanted to ask something. Annie watched them go, a knotted sensation in her stomach.

"You said you work with the detective?" Mrs. Turner asked timidly, breaking the silence.

Annie turned back to her. "Yes."

"Then you know... Isabella might not have been the first woman killed by that monster." Mrs. Turner searched her expression.

Annie winced. "I... can't comment at this time."

Mrs. Turner took hold of her wrist. "It's all right. I'm not asking for details like my husband. I want a promise from you. Find those other girls. Their parents deserve to give them a proper burial."

"We will do the best we can," Annie promised her. She glanced over at Adam, whose expression was torn between sorrow and sympathy. Determination welled in her. *And we will use every means we can as well.*

CHAPTER THREE

WHEN SOMEONE TAPPED HER SHOULDER, Annie was at the local plant nursery, hoping to find the ingredients she needed for some potions. She nearly jumped out of her skin and whirled. Her heart thudding jumped up another notch when she saw who it was—Adam.

Clearing her throat, she swatted his arm. "What are you doing, sneaking up on me like that?"

"Sorry." Adam held his hands in surrender, but an impish smile crossed his face. "You looked so lost in thought that I decided to see if you were Astro-projecting.

Annie was so happy to see that the heavy cloud smothering him at the funeral had lifted. She rolled her eyes at him but smiled in return. It had been a couple of days since they last talked. Adam was busy investigating the physical leads and continuing to interrogate Jonathan Swift while Annie looked more into her visions and how to get them back.

"I was heading to your house when I saw your car out front." Adam nodded toward the exit of the store.

"You were? Why didn't you call me?"

"I did, several times. It's why I was heading over there. I was worried about you."

Annie pulled her cell phone from her pocket and grimaced. "Sorry, I forgot to charge it last night; I've been scattered these last couple of days."

Adam nodded. They started down the aisle again. Annie breathed in the rich scent of earth and fresh greenery. She paused at a chocolate mint plant and picked it up. The potent scent hit her in the back of the throat, creating a pleasant coolness.

"These things are amazing," she told Adam, showing him the label. "They have such a powerful flavor. All you need to do is suck on one leaf, and it lasts. Better than chewing gum."

"I'm not overly fond of chocolate and mint together."

Annie laughed. "It doesn't really taste like chocolate." She put the plant into her basket. "See if you can find some hibiscus and stinging nettles, will you?"

Adam's brow scrunched. "I never thought you'd use such common plants in a witches' brew."

"There's more to potions than just these plants. You could put together something exactly as I do, but without the spells, it's just a delicate tea." Annie picked up a thyme plant and sniffed its leaves. It smelled a little dusty and old, so she put it back. "I talked with Rosemary a few times since we last saw watch other."

"Did she give you any help?"

"She gave me some hints about maybe jumpstarting the visions again. She suggested that something personal is holding me back from connecting with the lives of the women we're looking for."

"It's not a seance?" Adam asked.

Annie frowned at him. "Why are you so hung up on that? Seances are perfectly normal. Many cultures call on their ancestors for help, and a seance is one way of doing it. It's not all hokey chants and fake mumbo jumbo."

"I didn't mean it like that. I just… don't want you to get yourself in trouble, okay?" Adam's cheeks flushed as he grabbed a strawberry plant. He turned it around in his hands before holding it up. "You know, you have some magnificent property. You could probably grow a bunch of this yourself. I could build you some raised garden boxes if you want."

Annie wasn't sure how to answer that. She wondered if he was changing the subject or making the offer for another reason. "Uh, sure. That would be great. I've been meaning to put in a garden, but with all the cases we've had, I guess I haven't taken the time."

"We'll figure out a time for that, then. In the meantime, would you like to join me in interviewing the families of the missing women? I've narrowed the potential victims to five whom I believe are certainly Swift's victims." Adam put the strawberry plant back.

Annie considered it as she moved down the next row, then shook her head sadly. "I don't think it will do any good. I'm not good at reading people, and Rosemary says I need to eliminate distractions. So that's what I'm doing."

She wouldn't admit it, but there was more than just hearing the victims' families and seeing their grief that would distract her. It was happening more and more that Adam would intrude on her thoughts. His kind smile, sparkling eyes, and teasing lilt to his voice. She'd always found him attractive, but something was getting stronger these days.

Shaking her head, she resumed her search. "I can't let myself be distracted. You follow the evidence. I'll bring the magic."

It was nighttime before the potions were ready. She had prepared a concentration brew, a relaxation brew, a mind-clearing potion, and then five connection potions. There was one connection potion for each of the women who had disappeared. She had the names and faces of the ones Adam thought Swift had also killed.

Despite her potions, Annie still felt a distant sort of anxiety. If the potions worked and connected her to the murdered women, she would, at best, witness their deaths. At worst, she would live through them.

Don't let yourself be distracted; she reminded herself. Her inner voice sounded oddly like Rosemary's.

Thinking about her mentor released some of the tension she carried.

Centering herself once more, Annie picked up the first missing person's report. It was the most recent of the missing women... the most likely to be found alive, however unlikely it was.

Monty had been nowhere to be found all day, and Annie was grateful for the solitude. Her candles were lit in a circle around her, lighting her surroundings as she opened the file. Yasmine Delisle. She was married with two children. She volunteered at soup kitchens, and her disappearance was initially thought to be connected to a recent rash of drug-related crime in the area.

Her husband still lived in the apartment Yasmine's parents had gifted the newlyweds for their wedding in Chicago. He worked from home part-time as an editor while taking care of their children. The two of them were, by all accounts, happily married. He offered a reward for any information linked to her disappearance.

Annie turned the page and read the details of her abduction. She was an elementary school teacher and left work one day to deal with a problem at the soup kitchen where she volunteered. She never made it to the kitchen and never returned to work. Her journals spoke of some dissatisfaction with her current situation but were full of love for her husband and children. No sign she was planning to leave. No indication that she was afraid for her life.

The last person to have seen her alive was one of her seven-year-old students, except for her abductor.

"I'm sorry for your pain, Yasmine," Annie said out loud. Rosemary told her it might help to talk to the person she was trying to find as though they were in the room with them. "You must be so worried about your husband and children. I want to help you. I want you to find peace."

Annie lapsed into silence. What more could she say? She slid the photograph of Yasmine out and set the file aside. Then, she reached into another file and found Jonathan Swift's mugshot. As she looked at his picture, a shudder ran down her spine. He looked like a completely normal person. Average. Not very attractive, but not unattractive, either.

Something in his eyes made her senses rub raw, though. Or maybe it was only because she knew what he was capable of.

"You, I don't want to connect to," she told the photo. "But if it means finding Yasmine and the other women, I will. You are a terrible person. I will find them, though. You can't stop me."

She set the two pictures down side by side and picked up her first connection potion. She put it on the floor between the pictures and dipped her fingers into it. Sprinkling the potion on the two photos, she murmured spells under her breath. Finally, she picked up Yasmine's picture and put it on fire with a lighter. As flames licked up the side of the photo, Annie caught the ash in her potion.

Once the fire consumed the picture, she drank the potion and lay on the floor. The light from the candles seemed to sway on either side of her as she stared up and concentrated on the mental image of Yasmine's face.

"You shouldn't be here."

Annie's eyes snapped open. She bolted upright, gasping in surprise. This wasn't in her bedroom. She sat on a sidewalk, but the world around her seemed hazy. It shifted and pulled around her. Annie scrambled to her feet, looking around.

She gasped when she saw the woman standing next to her. "Yasmine?"

Yasmine stared at her. "You shouldn't be here."

"Where is here?" Annie asked, looking around.

"Chicago. I'm trying to find my home, but I'm stuck here." Yasmine pointed toward a house labeled *4738*.

"Is this where he took you?"

"Who?"

"Jonathan Swift."

Yasmine only kept staring at the house without a reaction. "I tried to be a good wife—a good mother. I tried. But I felt like I was failing at every turn. I wish I could see them one last time. I want... tell my husband I'm not in pain."

Annie rubbed her arms. It was only now that she realized how cold she was. When she looked down at herself, she saw a thin layer of frost building on her skin. Her breath puffed out in a misty cloud.

"Tell them," Yasmine murmured, but her voice seemed to come from far away. "Promise me."

Annie fell to her knees, too cold to stand. She felt her eyes freeze over and screamed, her voice echoing in the shifting world as it tore her throat.

CHAPTER FOUR

ANNIE'S BACK BENT, pain shooting through her as she screamed. She bolted upright, finding herself on her bedroom floor once more. The candles she'd lit the previous night were nothing more than puddles of wax now; each one melted out and then hardened again. The curtains, closed the previous night, were pulled apart, and the window was open.

"What?" Annie murmured. Her throat was raw and hurt as she got to her feet.

Her legs wobbled, and she sat back down. Now that she was growing more aware of herself, she was full of aches and pains, as though she had been beating herself against the floor. The time she had spent in the dream was so short, yet hours had gone by.

A tiny scraping sound made her glance to her left. Monty sat on the floor, scraping his fingernails on the floor. Once he got her attention, he pointed at her and signed so rapidly that Annie couldn't keep up with his admonishing.

"Did you open the window?" Annie asked, attempting to stand again. She was freezing!

Monty scowled but nodded.

Interesting. When she first got to the cottage, Annie had to put a spell on the remote so Monty could watch TV and not get so bored. He was getting more proficient in interacting with the world of the living without the spells.

"I didn't think you cared," Annie teased over her shoulder as she reached the window. She slid them shut and then sat back on her bed.

When she glanced at Monty, his scowl was even deeper. *I don't want any newbies moving into the home. You're barely tolerable as it is.*

Annie couldn't help but laugh. Her head throbbed, though, so she groaned as she lay back. "I'm fine. I need a little rest to get over it. Thank you, Monty."

No response. But Monty was gone when she glanced at where he had been sitting. Annie smiled to herself as she pulled a blanket up to her chin and let her eyes flutter shut. Living with him really was like living with a cat, she mused. He acted all aloof and like he didn't care, but when it came down to it, he did.

Annie slept for another three hours, but when she woke the second time, the aches and pains were gone. She felt alert and full of energy.

Remembering how her inability to answer her phone yesterday worried Adam, the first thing she did was check to see if she had missed any messages. Nothing. She wasn't sure if she was disappointed or not by that.

"No time to dwell on that," she told herself briskly as she jumped out of bed.

Within a few minutes, she was in her car, driving to the police station. The details of her vision remained crisp in her mind as she found a parking spot and headed in. The officers were used to seeing her consult with Adam, so they nodded to her in greeting as she made her way to the office that had 'Detective Parker' written on it.

Annie didn't even think about knocking before she breezed in. "We're going on a road trip," she declared.

Adam sat at his desk. His usually unruffled appearance was disheveled. Pictures and files lay on his desk in an organized grid pattern, and he held a half-empty cup of coffee. Five o'clock shadow was starting to darken his chin and cheeks.

"What are you talking about?" he asked, sounding exhausted.

"Have you been awake all night?" Annie asked in worry. She closed the office door.

Adam grunted, looking a little embarrassed. "Not entirely. But I don't have the brainpower to be productive."

"I'll drive, and you can have a nap. I'll also buy you breakfast and fresh coffee when we get there," Annie decided.

"Where?" Adam asked. An edge of irritation entered his voice.

Annie shook her head, grimacing. Right. She had forgotten entirely that he didn't know everything she did. "I performed a ritual last night—"

Adam straightened, an alarmed look on his face.

"I didn't call on the dead at all," she said quickly, even though that wasn't entirely true. He didn't need to know all the details. "I was able to force a vision last night, and I could see some things. I think I know where Yasmine Delisle is."

Adam put down his coffee and stood, grabbing his suit jacket off the back of his chair. "You saw where she's buried?"

Annie let out a shuddering breath. "Not exactly. I don't think Swift buried her... at least, not yet. So, let's go; I don't want to leave her there any longer than we already have."

Something flitted across Adam's expression, but he only nodded once as he gestured for her to lead the way out of the office.

It took them a little over five hours to get to Chicago. Adam fell asleep before they even hit the highway, and though Annie wanted to tell him everything she had discovered, she also wanted to let him rest. He looked so exhausted.

In the end, she put a spell over his area of the car to keep from hearing the noise, then put on some upbeat music to keep her awake. He woke up naturally just before they reached the city, and Annie turned off the music before she removed the surrounding spell.

"Need some breakfast and coffee?" she asked brightly.

Adam rubbed his eyes. "That would be great—my treat, okay?"

"Sure thing."

"I can't believe how hard I slept. Guess this beetle isn't as uncomfortable as I feared." He gave her a bit of a lopsided grin before he settled back in the seat. "So, are you going to tell me what happened now?"

Annie hesitated. She wasn't entirely sure how to describe what had happened to her the previous night. She certainly didn't want to tell Adam—she didn't want him to worry about her. So, she finally just shrugged. "I induced another vision and found a house where I believe Yasmine's body is. First, though, we have to find a funeral home."

Adam frowned. "Funeral home?"

"Meadowlark Funerals and Caskets," Annie rambled off, rolling her shoulders. The long drive had left her muscles tight and sore again.

"That sounds familiar... isn't that the funeral home Jonathan Swift went through for his wife's funeral?" Adam's jaw tightened visibly, and Annie could see that he was upset by this news. "I should have investigated them. They're connected to the killings?"

Annie sorted through the details of her vision again. She had seen the sign for the funeral home, but unlike 4738, she hadn't felt a sense of dread about it. If anything, the funeral home provided a sense of peace. She wasn't sure what to expect there.

"I think it will give us answers," she finally said.

After getting some food, they headed to the funeral home. A faint mist hung in the air despite it being mid-afternoon. Brick buildings lined the streets, and in the shimmering light, it looked like they had stepped back in time. The sidewalks were empty, and other than a few birds sitting on the roofs of the stores, it looked utterly deserted.

"It's kind of spooky," Adam noted as they headed toward the funeral home's doors.

Annie shook her head. "No. It's peaceful. It's just the sort of place a troubled spirit would go to overcome the trauma of her death."

Adam gave her a concerned look but said nothing.

Inside the funeral home, an elderly woman sat at the reception. She had lovely silver-blue hair and wore a cozy, hand-knit cardigan wrapped around her frail frame. Annie smiled at her as she stepped up to the desk.

"Hello," she greeted. "I'm Annie, and this is my friend, Detective Adam Parker. Could we have a few minutes of your time?"

The receptionist stared at her blankly while Adam cleared his throat.

"Who are you talking to?" Adam asked.

"The..." Annie trailed off as she inspected the receptionist. Her skin was almost luminous, and the silvery tones to her weren't because of old age at all. She blushed. "Oh, I am sorry."

Adam touched her wrist. "Annie?"

She turned to him, shaking her head. "There's a spirit here. I mistook her for a receptionist."

"I am, of sorts," the woman said as she stood. "Sorry, most people don't see me. Hold on, dear, I'll go get Robert."

"Thank you," Annie said hesitantly.

The ghost floated through the wall, and Annie turned to Adam. His expression was hard and suspicious. She hated seeing him look like that. "You believe me, don't you?"

"I... want to believe," Adam hedged.

Annie's stomach plummeted. He thought she was a liar. Did this mean that every time he called her *Little Witch*, it was teasing? She thought he believed in her magic, but was he pretending all this time?

She didn't have the chance to ask, as at that moment the ghost returned, through the door to the back this time. Seconds later, the door opened, and a middle-aged man with greying hair and bright, intelligent eyes entered.

"Hello," he greeted. He leaned on an elegant cane as he walked over and offered his hand to Adam. "I'm Robert Jenson. How may I help you?"

CHAPTER FIVE

ADAM LOOKED SUSPICIOUSLY over the mortician, though he fought to keep his expression smooth and emotionless. He trusted Annie too much to believe she was trying to pull the wool over his eyes, but everything was just so exhausting.

After he failed to save Isabella Turner, he didn't want to think about spirits wandering the world, lost. Adam wasn't exactly a religious guy, but he believed in heaven. His heart ached to think that a young woman who had already lost so much at the hands of Jonathan Swift would be lost from heaven simply because he hadn't arrived in time to save her.

Was it even possible to be barred from eternal rest? Shouldn't only those who have to make up for their past mistakes have the unrest of wandering about the Earth, unable to move on?

He shook his head slightly. Robert looked perfectly respectable. He had kind eyes and a resting smile that would put mourners at ease.

"Have you ever done business with a man named Jonathan Swift?" Adam asked.

"Jonathon?" Robert's brows furrowed. "Yes, actually. We handled his wife's funeral some six years ago. He comes in on the anniversary of her death every year to buy another casket."

Annie leaned forward, but her eyes were on the space beside Robert. "Don't you find that strange?"

Robert turned, and they both watched the blank space before Robert nodded. "That's right."

"What is?" Adam asked, fighting back the irritation.

Annie winced. "Sorry. I forgot to tell you. Adam can't see spirits."

Adam's gaze roved the empty room. "There's someone with us?"

"My mother, Gertrude," Robert offered.

"A spirit," Adam clarified.

Annie slid her hand into his and squeezed. He appreciated the physical comfort—his head was spinning. He squeezed back, giving her a small, thankful smile. But his heart was heavy. Had Isabella moved on? Or was she still trying to find her way?

"Yes. She only passed recently and wanted to make sure Robert got himself taken care of before moving on." She paused, then nodded. "Jonathon told them he was buying the caskets to give to other young families who unexpectedly lost a loved one. They didn't find it strange because it seemed like a sweet tradition."

Adam processed the information as he pulled a picture from his pocket and showed it to Robert. "Have you seen this woman? Her name is Yasmine Delisle?"

"Yasmine?" Robert's brow furrowed, and he shook his head. "I can't recall seeing her before. Mother?"

Adam glanced at Annie, who shook her head slightly.

It wasn't the news he wanted to hear. As far as his investigation had told him, Jonathon had lived with his wife just outside of the city. He moved around to find his victims, so he still had no proof that Jonathon had taken Yasmine... nor was he any closer to finding where she was buried.

"Did you notice anything strange out of the ordinary?" Annie urged, looking from the space to Robert. "Anything you might think of will be helpful to know."

Robert clucked his tongue. "Come to think of it, yes. He recently had an order for another casket, even though the anniversary of his wife's passing was already over."

Adam's heart gave a sudden, hard thump. "How many has he bought over the years?"

"Seven or eight, I should think," Robert said. He looked between Adam and Annie. "I'm sorry, but I'm baffled about what is happening here. Is Jonathon in some sort of trouble? And why did you say he *claimed* to be giving them to other families?"

Annie blew a heavy breath and looked at Adam, her eyes pleading. She was so bright and full of life; it was hard for her to express these things. Adam, unfortunately, had far more experience.

"Jonathan Swift was recently taken into custody for the murder of a young woman named Isabella Turner. I believe he has had at least five other victims. Knowing how many caskets he purchased from you may help us find the bodies of the other woman." He kept his expression neutral, his tone calm. People didn't respond well to any emotion in these sorts of circumstances.

Annie nodded once. "It's unfortunately true. I contacted Yasmine in my dreams last night, and she led me here. It's why I was hoping you'd have seen her.

Robert, looking distinctly shaken, headed for the computer at the reception. "Hold on; I can get you my records. I can't believe it. Jonathon seemed like such a nice young man... deeply mourning his wife but...."

He sat at the computer and rapidly typed on it.

"Thank you," Adam said.

Robert printed the sales records and handed them over to Adam. "Eight. He bought eight caskets from us, starting six years ago with his wife."

Adam's heart hammered even harder into his ribs. He barely thanked Robert again before he turned on his heel and strode away. Annie raced after him. Her expression was worried, her gaze never leaving his face.

"What is it?" she asked him.

"There's someone else."

Annie tossed him her keys and slid into the passenger side door. Adam had to adjust the position of the driver's seat before he got in after her. Annie had plugged a new address into the GPS by that time, and the electronic voice gave Adam directions.

"What do you mean, there's someone else?"

Adam's grip tightened on the wheel. "Eight caskets. One for his wife. Five for the missing women we've already connected to him. One for Isabella. That's only seven. We're missing someone. Someone he took before Isabella… or maybe after."

"But you arrested him on site, didn't you?" Annie asked, her eyes wide.

Adam's mind rushed in circles. "Isabella had been dead for about an hour when we found her. And Jonathon Swift was caught driving back into town. But with her injuries, Isabella could have been lying on that floor for days before she actually passed."

"Oh, Adam," Annie breathed. She twisted her hands together. "Yasmine didn't tell me anything about another person. But…"

Was there a chance? A seventh victim that could still be alive?

"Where are we going?" he asked his voice tense.

"To where he's keeping Yasmine." Annie shuddered visibly. "Adam…?"

Adam heard the question in her voice, but he had no room to answer. So he pressed harder on the gas, increasing their speed. Even though he knew chances were, they were already too late.

Annie kept feeling colder and colder as they grew nearer to their destination. When she recognized the buildings from her dream, her teeth began chattering. Pain throbbed through her stomach, and she bit back the urge to tell Adam to turn around, to take her away from here.

I have to do this, she reminded herself.

4738 was soon in view. Adam abruptly stopped in front of it and hurried around the car to open Annie's door. He helped her out, his expression concerned.

"Are you all right, Little Witch?'"

Annie made herself smile. "Yeah. Let's go in."

They headed up the driveway when suddenly, a figure melted through the doorway. Yasmine stood there; her hands clenched into fists. "Hurry!" she called.

Annie broke into a run.

"The key is under the mat," Yasmine said, pointing.

Annie kicked aside the mat and grabbed the key. She shoved it into the lock and opened the door before Adam caught up. The pain was getting worse. She was so cold she expected to see ice coating her skin. As she stumbled in, Yasmine hovered behind her.

"In the basement, behind the blue door," Yasmine said urgently

"Basement," Annie gasped, falling to her knees. "Blue door. Go!"

"Annie—" Adam said urgently.

"Go!"

Adam rushed past her. Yasmine stood where she was, looking anxiously down the dark stairs. A rush of warmth suddenly washed over Annie's frame. She sighed in relief, lifting her face.

"Call the ambulance," Yasmine told Annie. "She'll need it."

Annie dialed 9-1-1 without question, even though she could hardly speak.

One by one, five other women appeared. Tears hit Annie's eyes as she recognized each of Jonathon's victims. Last of all was Isabella Turner, with her arms wrapped around herself, watching the basement as Adam came back up, carrying a limp form in his arms.

"What...?" Annie asked, but as she blinked, the women were gone.

"She's alive," Adam said as he laid the limp figure onto the carpeted floor. He yanked off his coat and spread it over her. "He had her locked in a freezer room with their caskets. But she's alive, Annie... alive!"

CHAPTER SIX

ANNIE ACCOMPANIED the young woman to the hospital, while Adam stayed at the house to apprise the Chicago police of what was happening. The woman was nearly frozen to death and badly malnourished and dehydrated, but the doctors said she would make it.

After a few hours, Adam met Annie at the hospital. Jonathan Swift's six victims had disappeared except one. Isabella sat beside the young woman, watching her while Annie dozed in a chair.

Isabella wore a full-length black coat; the same one she had been wearing when Jonathan Swift took her. Annie recognized it now. It had been the one she saw on the mysterious figure who had left the wake quickly without talking to anyone. Isabella had been there; Annie just hadn't realized it at the time.

"I talked to the doctors," Adam murmured as he handed Annie a cup of coffee. "We got to her just in time. I wish Isabella had been as lucky... I wish I had found her in time."

Isabella looked up. "He blames himself? He shouldn't. I was going to die, anyway. I wasn't quite all the way gone when he got there. And I could see his sorrow. I didn't die alone because of him, and I will be forever grateful for that."

Annie took Adam's hand. She wasn't sure how he was going to take it. "Isabella's here."

Adam stiffened.

"She wants you to know that she doesn't blame you. She's just happy that you could find her. Your presence was a comfort to her as she died."

Adam still didn't relax.

"Did you find out her identity?" Annie asked, hoping to distract him.

"No. We searched the premises and found the other women in the caskets, but there was no sign of who this young woman is." Adam passed a hand over his eyes. "I hope she wakes soon so we can reunite her with her family."

Isabella seemed to fade somewhat, then came back into complete focus next to Adam's shoulder. "I know who she is."

Annie's hand tightened on Adam's reflexively. "Isabella knows her."

Adam's brow furrowed. "How?"

"Her name is Elizabeth Martinelli, and she's my twin sister. We were adopted," Isabella added, looking back to the sleeping form on the bed. "She didn't have a good life as I did. I contacted her, and we were talking, cautiously learning about each other, before that man...."

"They were twin sisters, given up for adoption," Annie explained to Adam. "They hadn't ever met, but I guess Swift must have gotten access to their records. Since they were both born the day his wife died, he went for both of them. Isabella was more like his wife, though, so he focused on her. Why would he have bought another casket for Elizabeth, though?"

Adam shook his head. "I don't think he was looking for his wife. At the house, we found a bunch of books on necromancy; I think he was trying to bring her back to life."

"Oh." Annie shifted closer to the detective, another shudder running down her spine.

She now understood that her vision connected her to Elizabeth rather than Yasmine. It had all been so confusing, but that was why she had been so cold and in pain. Even though the potion hadn't worked exactly as she wanted, she was still happy with the results.

A woman was alive now because of them. And that was all that mattered.

Several days later, with further evidence of Jonathan Swift's crimes and Elizabeth's testimony, he pleaded guilty and was sentenced to a life-time in prison with no parole. Annie was glad that such a dangerous man would never be on the streets again.

Isabella and the others moved on, or at least Annie thought they did. It made her wonder what was keeping Monty around. Maybe one day, she would ask him about it.

Today, though, she was already in his bad books. Adam was coming over for dinner, and Monty continually expressed his displea-sure by knocking things off the counter.

"Why don't you go watch a movie?" Annie complained as she picked up a pile of letters for the fifth time.

Monty narrowed his eyes at her and folded his arms.

"Adam believes you're here now," she added, hoping that would make a difference.

No such luck. He knocked a glass of water over. Annie bit back a curse as she rushed to mop up the water. Monty glared a moment longer before he stalked off through the wall. Annie huffed a breath, wishing she knew what was wrong with him.

Adam showed up a little while later, bringing a bottle of wine and a salad to go with the meatloaf and potatoes Annie had prepared. She quickly set the table, and Adam poured the wine as they sat up to eat.

"Do you want to talk about the Swift, or are you done for the day?" Annie asked him.

"We can talk about it. All the women he killed were identified and have been returned to their families for burial." Adam set the wine bottle down and smiled at her. He looked as though a great weight had been lifted off his shoulders. "And you? Any other visions?"

Annie shook her head. "It seemed like when I replaced all my spices and herbs; it got rid of whatever was tainting them to give me spontaneous visions. I'll keep working on the potion I used to find Elizabeth, though. It will be good to control these things."

Adam cut his meatloaf into bite-sized pieces. "But is it safe? We've never really talked about magic. At first, I thought you were playing, but this case has forced me to look at this. It's all real, isn't it?"

"Yes." Annie lowered her fork. "Did you think I was lying?"

"I tried not to think of it at all, if I'm honest."

"I see."

Adam must have heard the disappointment in her voice because he looked up quickly. "I never believed in any of this stuff, not even when I was a kid. I was a facts man. But you turn me upside down in more ways than one, Annie. Sometimes, I don't know what to do."

Surprise rippled through her. It was the last confession that she had expected tonight. Butterflies erupted in her stomach. "I... don't always know what to do around you, either. I thought you would dismiss me when I said I was a witch. But you trust me. That... means a lot."

Her fingers crept across the table toward him.

"Well... I'm still waiting," he said gruffly, his usually calm demeanor broken by the blush on his cheeks. "Are these potions safe?"

"Yes," Annie said promptly.

And they were... mostly. Annie still had the occasional icy chill creep over her, but it never lasted long. Besides, there were bound to be some side effects of the potions. At least this way, she could monitor herself.

"I'd feel better if your mentor... Rosemary, was it?"

"Yeah."

"If she could come and give you a magical checkup, I don't know." Adam frowned as he chewed his meatloaf. "Do they have magical checkups?"

Annie laughed and waved a hand. "You're worrying too much, Adam. I'm perfectly fine. I know what I'm doing. Potions don't change a person; they open up the body's natural systems to be receptive to what is normally shut out."

Adam leaned forward. "Does that mean you could make a potion to make me have your visions instead?"

Annie drew back in shock. Was he being serious, or was this a test?

Was he seeing if it was safe, as she claimed? The truth was that she wouldn't give Adam a potion that hadn't been rigorously tested.

Concern twisted her stomach. Was she playing with forces beyond her power? She had been using her magic to help Adam solve his cases before she started having visions. Was it such a bad idea to take the potion to Rosemary and put it through some peer review? Was she taking unnecessary risks herself?

Prophecy can't be created. If it's invoking these visions, it just means it's opening up my mind enough to tap into an ability I already have. I need the potions to help me get to where I can tap into my visions without them.

She laughed as she playfully shoved Adam's shoulder. "Oh, I see what you're doing!"

"What?"

Annie gave him an impish grin as she sipped her wine. "You're hoping you can use my potions to give yourself visions and cut me out of the fun part."

"Hey," Adam protested. "That's not—"

"You want all the glory to yourself," Annie continued teasingly, "Detective Adam Parker, the new Sherlock Holmes. Cut out the middleman and receive the visions straight to your head."

Adam rolled his eyes. "Oh, I see how it is. You want me to keep begging you for help."

His tone took on a teasing lilt and Annie ignored the lingering worry in his eyes. She stood up and spread her arms as though addressing a massive crowd. "Ladies and gentlemen, I present you the dynamic detective duo. Annie and Adam! We'll solve your murder!"

Adam clapped. "Brava, brava!"

Annie bowed to him, happy that the conversation had turned. She retook her seat and tasted the salad. The dressing was creamy and sweet, with just a hint of sourness at the aftertaste. She grinned.

"This is delicious," she told Adam.

"Thanks. It's my grandmother's recipe."

Annie latched onto the topic. "How is she doing?"

"Up to her usual hijinks," Adam chuckled.

They fell into the familiar pattern of discussing family and plans for the next few days. Adam would be building that raised garden bed he promised on the weekend, and Annie was already plotting how she would plant the herbs from her garden.

At one point, Monty ducked into the dining room again. Annie pointed him out, and Adam greeted him politely, but Monty only left again without communicating. Annie made up some lies to make her roommate not seem rude, and the rest of the evening passed in laughter and fun.

Well, after dark, Adam decided it was time to go home. Annie walked him to the door, and he stood half in and half out. A beautiful full moon hung in the sky outside.

"I always loved the full moon," Adam whispered. He turned back to her and smiled at her. "Goodnight, Little Witch."

His hand came up, and he brushed his thumb over her cheekbone. Sparks tingled under her skin, and warmth blossomed from the place he touched her. Adam's eyes were in darkness, so that she couldn't see him. His fingers slid down her cheek, tucking under her chin. He lifted her face to his. For a moment, she thought he was going to lean forward.

But then his hand dropped, and he walked down the front path to his car. Her heart slammed into her chest, feeling off balance as Adam drove away. She touched her cheek where his warmth lingered, then turned back into her house.

A smile blossomed over her face. She locked the door and went to clean up the dining room. Another case successfully closed, a woman's life was saved, and a new potion she could use to save others. And best of all, a fantastic night with Adam Parker.

How could life get any better than this?

The End

AN ANNIE ARCHER PARANORMAL MYSTERY

THE CASE OF THE

UNLUCKY HANDYMAN

A COZY MYSTERY

DAISY LANDISH

CHAPTER ONE

A GHOSTLY SPECTER loomed in the black smoke with a hideous gash across its throat. Eyes narrowed in anger as one pale hand lifted to point. A harsh alarm wailed unceasingly.

Annie Archer, choking on the smoke, quickly unplugged the toaster. Then she grabbed a dirty cookie sheet by the sink to fan the fire alarm. After a few powerful swishes, the blaring alarm stopped. Annie fanned it a few more times before she dropped the cookie sheet back onto the counter.

"Don't look at me like that," she snapped at her ghostly roommate, Monty. That wasn't his real name, but he refused to tell her what it was, so she made a name for him. "It's not my fault this toaster is crapping out."

She dumped the blackened toast out, grimacing. She had put it on the lowest setting because this over-burnt toast had become a daily habit. The darn toaster must be broken, which was annoying since she would have to buy a new one.

"Ugh," Annie said as she tossed the toast. "Guess it's cold cereal for me again."

The oven wasn't working properly, either. Unfortunately, the beautiful little cottage she had bought after moving from Boston was riddled with problems, and they were stacking up. She wasn't sure how long her charms and potions could keep things running.

Magic wasn't a fix-all. It certainly helped with things like allowing Monty to watch TV at will, but it only took care of outdated wiring for so long.

With a sigh, Annie grabbed her day planner and jotted down a note to call an electrician. "I'm going to have someone look at the wiring," she said aloud. "I know you don't like strangers in the house, but this is getting dangerous."

She glanced at Monty. He scowled at her as he used sign language to say, *can't you get that cop to come to it? You have him over for everything else.*

"Adam isn't an electrician," Annie said. Before she and Monty took sign language lessons together, they hadn't been able to communicate well with the ugly gash across Monty's throat. "But does this mean you're starting to like him?"

Monty's scowl grew deeper, and he faded from sight. Annie had to giggle at that. As frustrating as it could be, she learned that Monty's penchant for disappearing meant she was getting too close to the truth for him.

Annie glanced sadly at her toaster before getting out a cereal box. Tomorrow she would have to remember to wake up a little earlier, so she could stop in at the diner for a good, hot breakfast before heading to her store.

A surge of warm, fuzzy feelings rushed through her. Her store. After leaving Boston, she had been at a loss for what to do. She'd been working as a receptionist at a security company for years, but it was never fulfilling. Recently, she landed on the idea of opening an antique store—all right; she got the idea from watching *Ghost Whisperer*, so sue her—and had spent the last few months intensely researching and working.

Today was the first day of the second week her store would be open. So far, it had been a bit of a slow start, but Annie was positive business would pick up. She had a lot of outstanding pieces, after all.

As she sat down to eat, her phone rang. Her heart jumped when she saw who was calling her—Detective Adam Parker. She'd helped him solve quite a few cases since moving here, but they had also become good friends.

Annie wished they could add "boy" and "girl" in front of them. The more time she spent with Adam, she daydreamed about walking down an aisle toward him, wearing a ballgown of white satin.

She pushed those thoughts aside, clearing her throat before she answered. "Hey, Adam. What's up?"

"Nothing good, I'm afraid. You know Kyler North?"

Of course, she did. He was the one whom she had planned to call about her electricity. Kyler worked all over town as a handyman. He had ten different trade certificates and could fix just about anything. A sliver of dread slid down her spine.

"Yes," she said cautiously. "What about him?"

"He's dead, and I will need your help on this one. It looks witchy."

Annie swallowed hard, her hands going cold. They had dealt with a wicked witch trying to poison the mayor about a year ago, but there had been nothing since then. "Witchy, how?"

"Ritualistic, maybe," Adam amended. "I don't know enough about it all to say. He was found in his apartment, impaled through the back with an old ladder which was then used to prop him up as though he was standing beneath it. The number thirteen is carved into his forehead, and pieces of a broken mirror were around his feet."

Annie covered her mouth at the description. Even though she had seen dead bodies, there was nothing like this before. Beneath a ladder? A broken mirror?

"A black cat was found sitting on the top of the ladder. It's been hissing and attacking anyone who tries to get close to the body."

Oh, this was not good.

"Are you still there?" Adam asked, sounding worried.

"Have you moved the body?"

"No, not yet. The cat won't let anyone near…, and I get this odd, eerie feeling when I enter that apartment. I'm sure something magical is happening. Could you come over? I hate to make you see it, but this worries me."

The chill running through Annie's body intensified. Adam was as cool as they came. Even when he was worried about something, he wasn't the sort to admit it. Something was going on here, and Annie didn't like it.

"I have to stop by the shop first and put up a sign to say I'm not opening today," she said. Her voice trembled even though she fought against it. "I'll be there as soon as I can."

When Annie arrived at the apartment building where Kyler lived, she was unsurprised to find dozens of police cars outside and a good portion of the building's residences. Most of the uniformed police were taking notes in their conversations with the people, many of whom looked extremely shaken.

Annie got out of her car, fingering the bracelet in her pocket. She couldn't be too careful if this were related to magic.

The uniform guarding the apartment building entrance was someone she recognized, though she couldn't remember his name. He had a clipboard with her name and escorted her to the top floor, where Adam waited for her.

"Thanks, Steve," Adam said to the uniformed officer with a nod. "You can go back to the door."

Steve nodded once and pressed the elevator button to take him back to the main floor.

Adam was dressed in his usual business suit, his hair well-groomed and his face clean of all stubble. Faint whiffs of cologne wafted off him. Annie was more drawn to the nerves that clearly showed in the tightness of his jaw and the way his shoulders were set.

Goosebumps rose on her arms and her scalp prickled as her nerves seemed to set on fire, sending warning signals to her brain.

"You're right. There's magic here," she whispered, then pulled the bracelet from her pocket. She pressed it into Adam's hand. "I want you to wear this until the case is over. Don't take it off, not even to sleep and shower."

Adam inspected the bracelet. "A four-leaf clover?"

"It brings luck to combat the bad luck of whatever is going on here," Annie explained. "And this is the Hand of Hamsa, which is for protection. I don't like the energy here. Please, trust me on this one, okay?"

Even though Annie considered herself a good witch who used her magic to help others, she was still versed in dark magics, at least identifying and protecting against them.

Adam slipped the bracelet on. Almost instantly, his tense muscles visibly relaxed. He looked at it in surprise.

"See?" Annie murmured.

"Kyler's apartment is this way. The M.E., Dr. James, is inspecting the body."

Adam led her down the hallway. The bad feeling in Annie's gut increased with every step she took, and she wished she had brought more potent protective charms. Well, she'd have a chance once she got home.

"Dr. James," Annie whispered.

"No last name?"

"Gross."

"What?" Annie's eyebrows furrowed. "What did I do?"

Adam gave her a smirk. "No, I mean his last name is Gross. James Gross. He prefers to go by his first name."

Annie's brows shot straight up, disappearing beneath her fringe bangs. She nearly laughed aloud. What a name for a medical examiner! As they got to the door, she shook her head, and Adam held the warning tape up for her to duck under.

She held her breath as she stepped into the apartment, but there was no sign of the body just yet, to her relief. A man wearing a white biohazard suit sat on a footstool, tending to claw marks on his hand. A torn glove lay discarded nearby.

"Dr. James," Adam called. "I'd like you to meet Annie. She's who I was telling you about."

James lifted his head and grinned. "Ah, the little witch. I'm pleased to meet you at last—Adam won't stop singing your praises. I must say, you live up to the legend."

He winked at her.

Annie smirked at that, shaking her head. Some men just had too much flirtatious energy in them. "Pleased to meet you, too. Now. Where's this black cat? We've got to get close to the body if we're going to solve this murder."

CHAPTER TWO

DR. JAMES LOOKED at her with worried eyes. "I'm not sure that's a good idea, Little Witch."

Annie stiffened. "Did you just call me Little Witch?"

"I…" James winced. "I shouldn't have, then?"

Annie shook her head, frowning. Only Adam called her Little Witch. Nobody else. "Please refer to me by my name. I'm Annie or Ms. Archer if you like."

"I'm sorry," James said. He looked contrite enough.

"Thank you."

"Well." James cleared his throat. "Anyway, it's a pretty grisly scene. Wouldn't you rather wait until I got the cat out of there?"

Annie shook her head again. She didn't want to wait any longer in this place with its dark feelings. As she glanced around the room, looking for clues about where the dark magic was coming from, her eyes landed on a framed picture on the coffee table.

Adam was telling James that Annie was an official consultant and not to question her, so Annie took the opportunity to step closer to the picture. It looked undisturbed, but she still pulled on a pair of gloves before picking up the picture. It was of a smiling old woman sitting in a rocking chair. And peeking into the frame were two black ears.

"It's his cat," she said.

Adam and James looked over at her. She showed Adam the picture.

"He told me he didn't like cats," Annie continued. "More of a dog person and his apartment wouldn't allow pets, anyway. But look, this is a picture of his mother, who has a black cat. I bet he took it in after she died."

"Is this a vision?" James asked doubtfully.

Adam glared at him. "I told you not to question her."

Annie was glad he was being protective, but she put a hand on his arm to calm him. "It's okay. He hasn't worked with us before. And no, it's not a vision. I could be entirely wrong about this. It just seems to be what's right."

"There's no litter box in the apartment," Adam said reluctantly.

"Then I guess I'm wrong." Annie shrugged. She didn't feel like she was, but maybe that was just nerves. She took a deep breath as she headed for the bedroom, where the body was found. "Let's get this over with."

The scene was exactly as Adam had described it. Annie did her best not to look too closely at the body. The black cat still sat on the top of the ladder. It was thin, but not so much that it looked like it was starving. Big yellow eyes narrowed in on her, and its fur stood on end. It yowled a warning.

"From what I can tell without a more thorough examination," James said as he edged around to the left, "a stab wound through the back to the heart killed the victim instantly. Everything else was done postmortem."

Annie watched the cat as its tail flicked back and forth, uncertain if it wanted to attack her or James. "How can you tell?"

"The glass from the mirror looks like it was arranged on purpose, and there is no blood from the wounds where the victim is propped into the ladder or on his forehead." James folded his arms as he eyed the cat warily. "My rough estimate would be he died ten to fifteen hours ago, but I'll know more once I can do a proper examination."

Adam touched Annie's elbow. "Think you can do anything?"

Annie watched the cat; it was only paying attention to her and James now. As she looked closer, she realized Adam had the same ash-brown hair as Kyler. He was even wearing his glasses today; usually, he just had contacts. Kyler also wore glasses.

"I think if James and I leave the room, you might get the cat down," Annie told him. "You look a little like Kyler."

Adam looked a bit unsettled to hear that, but he nodded. James and Annie left the room and stood on either side of the open doorway. Annie listened as Adam talked to the cat in a low, soothing voice. It was only a few minutes before he came out of the room, cradling the cat in his arms.

"Yes!" James crowed. He hurried back into the bedroom with his medical kit.

The cat snuggled into Adam's chest, purring. He kept his head tilted up, away from the animal. "Can you take it?" he whispered. "I'm allergic."

Annie crept forward. "Hey there, buddy."

The cat cracked one eye open, hissed, and snuggled tighter to Adam.

"Sorry," Annie said. "I don't think he'd accept me touching him. But if you want, we can take him back to my place… poor thing is traumatized, and it's nice and quiet there. I'm sure Monty won't mind."

Adam chuckled. "I thought you said he was like a cat himself. Aren't you afraid he'll get territorial, little—" He cut himself off abruptly, his face falling. "Sorry. I didn't realize you dislike being called that."

"By James," Annie was quick to protest. She moved closer again, her gaze intent on Adam. "I like you calling me Little Witch. You're the only one."

Adam stared at her. She thought she saw something stirring in his eyes, but James stuck his head back out of the bedroom as he opened his mouth. "What sort of toxicology analysis should I prepare to run?"

Adam frowned, but Annie shook her head. "I'll send you a list. A handful of substances become poisonous when combined with dark magic that would otherwise be safe."

"Righto," James said with a nod.

"Do you suspect the victim was subdued before being killed?" Adam asked.

"I can't tell just yet," James said. "But even stabbed through the back, there should be some signs of struggle. I'll know more when I'm able to complete the autopsy."

Annie nodded her understanding. Kyler was a vigorous man. He wouldn't have just sat around idly waiting for someone to stab him in the back. So, either it was a complete surprise, he knew and trusted his killer, or something had prevented him from fighting back. Given the lack of blood in the other room, he wasn't killed here.

"We'll get the rest of the techs in to help you," Adam said, his face scrunched up.

It was clear he was trying hard not to sneeze, and Annie quickly pulled a mint out of her pocket. She unwrapped it and put a hasty spell on the candy before popping it into Adam's mouth. His eyes widened in surprise as her fingertips brushed his lips. Annie felt a jolt go through her and her breath caught in her throat.

It was surprising what impact a simple touch could have.

Annie pulled back quickly, blushing. "Uh, I put a spell on that to help with your allergies. You're welcome."

James looked between them, understanding dawning in his eyes. He grinned wickedly but ducked back into the bedroom, saying nothing. Annie groaned. Hopefully, the new ME wasn't the sort of person to spread rumors about what he had just seen... not that there was anything to spread rumors about.

"I guess we should head down," Annie said briskly. But as she headed for the door, blushing still, she suddenly stopped dead.

It was as though a giant had reached into her lungs and squeezed. She couldn't breathe. Her hands and legs wouldn't move. She tried to gasp out to Adam and ask for help, but no sound left her lips. Her eyes bulged as she fought against the dark feeling pressing down on her.

"Annie?" Adam grabbed her arm.

Annie pulled in a big gasp, the sensations releasing her at once. She stumbled slightly, holding onto Adam for support. The car growled at her but stayed firmly in Adam's grip.

"He was paralyzed," Annie murmured as she hurried to escape this room. The dark magic had dissipated by this time, but it still left her with a terrifying feeling in the pit of her stomach. "And I'm certain they're a witch. You can't find these sorts of spells in a corner store. They much have used paralytic drugs... maybe a plant extract or a potion."

"Never mind that," Adam said, sliding his arm around her waist. She was still wobbly. "Are you okay? It looked almost like you had a vision."

"I can't have visions like that anymore," Annie said weakly.

She had been seeing visions of their victims for a while, but it was only because a rival witch in town had been drugging her. Now, she had to create a series of potions to induce a vision. It was hard on her body, though, so they only used them as a last resort.

"Are you okay?" Adam repeated, and the worry in his voice was evident.

Annie managed a smile. "I'm all right now."

Adam didn't look entirely convinced, but he nodded. "So, about the case. Who would know how to do this sort of thing? Other than a witch, I mean."

"A herbalist." Annie made herself straighten. Though she would have liked to continue to lean against Adam, the cat was getting more agitated with her proximity, and she didn't want the poor thing to bolt. "I have someone I can call. She's extremely knowledgeable. If anyone can figure out what happened here, it's her."

"Is she safe for you to talk to? Do you want backup?"

Annie was surprised at the depth of concern in Adam's voice. They stepped into the elevator, and she turned to him. "Don't worry. I'll be fine."

"This case isn't normal," Adam said, lowering his voice. "I don't want you to get hurt."

"I don't want you to get hurt, either," Annie whispered.

She searched his gaze, looking for signs of what he was feeling. She couldn't read the emotions on his face, however. Eventually, he nodded.

"Just call me if you need me," he said.

"I will. I promise."

CHAPTER THREE

WHEN THEY GOT the tox report back from James, Annie knew she had to visit Rosemary in person. Rosemary avoided her calls or cut the conversation short before Annie had a chance to ask her questions. It didn't give her a good feeling. Annie was confident her mentor would know something about this, but getting her to talk seemed to be a problem.

She was also sure that Rosemary would give excuses for not visiting, so Annie didn't tell her she was driving out to Portland to talk. It was a few hours of driving, and by the end, Annie wished she had taken up Adam's offer to drive her out here.

But Rosemary wouldn't say anything in front of a non-witch; besides that, some things just had to be done solo. Not to mention Adam still had to investigate the non-magical possibilities back home.

It was a little past midnight when Annie pulled into Rosemary's driveway. As expected, the house was all lit up, inside and out. Rosemary was the only witch Annie knew who put up Christmas decorations and kept them all year. The lawn was filled with Santa Clauses, reindeer, penguins, and giant, glowing snowflakes.

Annie had to smile, shaking her head. Most witches didn't celebrate Christmas at all; they celebrated the solstice as appropriate to their cultures, but Rosemary always said she would not pass up a jolly fat man dressed in red just because some people might not like her practices.

The woman herself opened the door before Annie even reached it. Her smile was big, as was usual with the older woman. She pulled Annie into a big hug.

"Why didn't you tell me you were coming? I would have had something for you to eat. What are you doing all the way to Portland? Where's that handsome detective fellow you're so insistent is just a friend?" Rosemary stepped back, her hands staying on Annie's shoulders. She clucked her tongue and shook her head. "You, my girl, haven't been sleeping. Is it that ghost of yours?"

Annie couldn't help but laugh. Visiting Rosemary was just like visiting a grandmother. "Could you at least let me come in before you bombard me with the questions?"

"Oh, of course." Rosemary stood aside and waved her in. "I just finished my coffee, getting ready for my midnight gardening. How is your herb garden going? You told me that this Adam Parker man would build you garden boxes, right?"

Annie toed off her shoes; Rosemary was a stickler for cleanliness. "The garden is doing well. Adam built me some garden boxes. We aren't a couple, and I haven't been sleeping well, but not because of Monty."

"Oh?" Rosemary took Annie's jacket and hung it up. "What then?"

"The little antique store I opened up. I've been busy getting everything ready."

"Why are you here, then? You should be at home getting ready for tomorrow." Rosemary tilted her head to one side, studying Annie. "Unless you were hoping to get permission from the Society to use a little magical advertising?"

Rosemary was the head of the witches' ethical committee for this side of the country, known as the Society. She was more than qualified. Her magical remedies completely revolutionized practical medicine among witches and non-witches. She had a knack for combing potions with spells and non-magical means of work.

"That's not why I'm here," Annie hedged.

"Ah. Let's get to the kitchen, and I'll find you something to eat."

Annie wasn't particularly hungry, but Rosemary's food was always delicious, so she followed silently. As Rosemary dug through her fridge, Annie considered what had brought her here.

The tox screen had returned negative for everything, including all the magical substances Annie had sent him to test for. The only conclusion was that it had metabolized quickly enough to dissolve even postmortem. Annie didn't like that. Rosemary was the only person she knew who was near talented enough to create something like this.

But why would Rosemary have to travel all the same to small town hours away just to poison Annie's handyman? Kyler had no connection with Rosemary, so why would she do it?

"I hired a manager to monitor the store on my days off," Annie said. She wasn't ready to outright accuse her mentor.

"Good. Because you look tired, dear. You need to stop taking so much on." Rosemary set a cold turkey sandwich in front of Annie. "I hope between this store and your work with Adam, you haven't been neglecting your studies. I noticed you haven't yet accepted your invitation to the Society's herbalist convention."

Annie picked up the sandwich and sniffed the warm bread. As fresh as the day it came out of the oven. "I plan to respond soon. But that's not why I'm here."

"Of course," Rosemary said as she slid into a chair next to Annie. "You're here because of the Bad Luck murder."

Annie sighed heavily. Of course, Rosemary would know, but she wasn't happy that this only made it more evident that Rosemary had been avoiding her. "I wouldn't have had to drive out here if you had just answered my questions over the phone."

"I don't think you had the right questions yet," Rosemary said delicately.

Annie took a bite of the sandwich to buy her time to think. She chewed thoughtfully as she watched Rosemary. In her time with Adam, she had learned to read people better. Rosemary seemed nervous, as though this wasn't a conversation she wanted to have. That wasn't a good sign.

"Have you ever heard of anything like this before?" Annie finally asked. "The broken mirror, the ladder, the black cat, the number thir-teen carved into his forehead. What could it mean?"

Rosemary clasped her hands over the table. "It means that whoever killed this man hated him desperately. Tell me about what you felt at the crime scene."

Annie shuddered. "It felt dark. There was magic there, all right, and it appeared it would poison me. When I was trying to leave, I suddenly became paralyzed."

"That is what I expected. From what you described, the killer set up a bad luck spell over the scene." Rosemary's gaze darkened. "But there's certainly the possibility that the spell wasn't meant for the victim."

"What?" Surprise rippled through Annie. She hadn't even consid-ered that before! "How could it not be for the victim?"

Rosemary gave her a stern glance. "You're a clever girl. What do you think?"

Annie frowned. But as she thought about it, the answer was obvi-ous. She could have kicked herself as the answer came. "Putting a bad luck spell on the investigators. First, the cat, sensing the negative ener-gies of the cops, wouldn't let them near his master. And if bad luck affects everyone on the case, it'll make it harder to solve the case."

"Exactly."

"I gave Adam a protective charm," Annie said anxiously. "It will keep him safe, right?"

Rosemary shook her head. "I'm not sure. It won't hurt to increase your protections for both him and you, however. I don't like the idea of any witches using dark magic, and certainly not to murder someone."

"I know what you mean. I'm certain that Kyler was paralyzed when he died. The M.E. couldn't find any traces of the substances I consid-ered. All his tests came back completely normal." Annie hesitated, unsure how to phrase this next part. "I have to conclude that it was a master herbalist at play."

Rosemary hummed, looking thoughtful.

"The most important thing is to find out what happened, though," Annie continued. "Do you have any suggestions on further tests we could run?"

Rosemary stood and headed for her stove. She filled a kettle with water, turned on the stove, and then turned back to her. "I'm making us both some tea. I'd like to add a bit of a restful spell to yours. It won't knock you out, but it will help you get a solid sleep the next time you go to bed."

Annie nodded once. It was ridiculous for her to even suspect Rosemary. One thing was sure; she trusted her mentor with her life.

As Rosemary prepared the tea, she spoke over her shoulder. "There's no point in wasting your time looking for whatever poisoned the young man. If he even was poisoned."

"But he was. I'm certain of it. The feeling I got was—"

"Perhaps put there on purpose to distract you. It's well known that you work with the police and that Detective Adam relies heavily on you."

Annie frowned. Was all this just a red herring, then? She turned it over in her mind as the kettle whistled. "I was wearing a protection, though."

"And you yourself know there are ways around it, especially since you have a predilection for visions."

Rosemary poured the tea into the cups and brought Annie's cup to her. The warmth from the hot liquid was already soothing.

There was no point in rushing Rosemary. She would get to her point here soon enough. Annie sipped her tea, watching her mentor as she put cream and sugar into her own tea. She was an elegant woman, with her silver hair pulled into a braid down her back as she wore an old cotton dress.

Returning to the table, Rosemary sat. "Now. Let me tell you what I think may have happened."

CHAPTER FOUR

ONCE ROSEMARY HAD SETTLED down again, she tapped her fingers against her teacup, a thoughtful look on her expression. Annie sipped her own tea. It was the perfect temperature, and she enjoyed the grassy flavor with floral notes. There was something extra special about a herbalist's tea.

"Now," Rosemary said, sipping her tea, "let's start with your assumption that the victim had been paralyzed before being stabbed. Please describe the exact sensations."

"I thought you would tell me what you thought happened," Annie complained.

"And I will... after you tell me this last thing." Rosemary sipped her tea, a sparkle in her eyes.

Annie huffed. Now she knew what it was like for Adam when she was caught up in her theories and didn't tell him what was happening until she was sure she had the right answer. She should probably apologize for that... this was infuriating.

"It didn't hit me until we were leaving," Annie said. "It felt like I suddenly couldn't move. My lungs wouldn't work; I couldn't even blink. It was as though someone had suddenly removed every bit of my willpower. It was terrifying."

Rosemary nodded. "As I thought. It was the effects of the Devil Doer."

Annie shivered. "What is that?"

"*Strychnos toxifera*. It's a plant found in several countries in South America. It is very useful in human-created drugs to treat certain ailments; however, when paired with certain magics and other herbs, it can become extremely potent." Rosemary shook her head. "I have some in my garden, in fact."

Annie chewed her lip. This wasn't good.

"I guess that whatever weapon was used to kill this man—"

"Kyler," Annie said.

Rosemary nodded. "Whatever was used to kill Kyler, it had a spell or potion on it. The bad luck charms were placed to keep the cops away, and, knowing that you help them out, no doubt another spell was placed in the area. Tell me, what did you do when you got there?"

"Nothing." Annie thought—that wasn't entirely true. "No, wait. I realized that Adam looked like Kyler and realized the cat wasn't afraid of him. So, I got the cat to move."

"Thus, triggering the spell to hit you." Rosemary nodded as though that solved it.

Annie was still confused, though. "But—"

Rosemary held up a hand. "The weapon had a spell put on it to kill Kyler. He didn't ingest any paralytics, but the killer set up a trap that would be active in the latent effects of their spell once you performed a certain action. It would have been much worse if you hadn't had your protection."

"So, they targeted me." Annie considered this for a moment. It was far more terrifying than she wanted to admit. If that were the case, the killer might come after her again to ensure she didn't figure out anything else. "But Kyler had no defensive wounds. How could he not have seen it coming?"

Rosemary arched a brow at her. "Witches, my dear. The weapon may have been animated with the sole purpose of killing Kyler. My guess would be it was made invisible by a spell."

"That doesn't bring me any closer to who it might be," Annie said. "Unless—does the Devil Doer have to be licensed to grow?"

Rosemary nodded.

"Good, then! I can get a list of everyone licensed to grow it and see who might connect with Kyler. Which means this is a witch matter. I will have a hard time convincing Adam to let me handle this on my own." Annie shook her head. "He's been pretty overprotective lately."

"Have you told him this?"

Annie hesitated. "Well.... No. I kind of like that he's been protective."

"Then why call him overprotective if you like it?"

Annie blew out a breath and sipped her tea. Rosemary had an amused smile—clearly, she guessed what was happening. And that wasn't exactly what Annie had in mind when she had come here. Another time, sure, she would have liked to discuss these blossoming feelings she had for Adam.

On the other hand, Rosemary was still a suspect in this case.

"Well?" Rosemary pressed. "Are you going to answer?"

"No. I want to stick with this case. You talked about a spell being put on the weapon. How many spells are there that require Devil Doer in their creation?"

Rosemary looked at the ceiling, her eyes roving over the old tiles. "Hmmm. I can think of four right now. Three of them are purely medicinal and have safeguards built into the spell to prevent an overdose; you mess with those safeguards, and the spell won't work."

"And the fourth?"

Rosemary sipped her tea.

"Are you going to answer?" Annie pressed.

"The fourth," Rosemary said slowly, "is one I made myself. It requires a particular method of extraction that nobody else knows. However, it would fit everything you have described. I created it long ago when I learned my daughter's husband was abusing her. My anger held no bounds."

Annie's breath caught in her chest. Was Rosemary admitting to having killed someone?

"He was hit by a bus before I could work up the courage to cast the spell. I destroyed my notes at once, of course. I'm the only one who could know how to cast it."

Annie's eyes widened. "What are you saying?"

Rosemary studied her for a moment. "Annie, do you believe I killed that man?"

"From what you're telling me, nobody else could have done it. If it was your spell, one that you didn't share with anyone else...." Annie hid her face in her hands. Normally, Rosemary was the last person in the world she would think capable of murder. "What other explanation do you have?"

"I have no explanation for how someone may have gotten that particular spell, Annie. But I can assure you, and I didn't kill him. I had no reason to; besides that, I have been extremely busy with the Society. When was he killed?"

"Between six and eleven last night."

Rosemary hummed. "Well, I was at a convention giving a talk about growing your own herb garden and some easy homeopathic remedies that people can make without magic from five to eight, and then I had a late dinner with another chairman until nine. I can give you their contact information."

Annie nodded, hating that she had to follow up on an alibi for her mentor. "Adam will be happy to have that information. It still leaves two hours... you can't get to our town in that amount of time."

Relief flooded over her. She didn't doubt that Rosemary was telling the truth about all of this; she was just glad that she wouldn't have to tell Adam that Rosemary was a potential suspect! On impulse, she leaned over and hugged Rosemary.

"I'm sorry for suspecting you."

"Oh, my dear Annie. I could see the reluctance in your eyes." Rosemary patted her back. "When all is said and done, you had to know. You believe in truth far too much."

Annie dabbed at her eyes, which had filled with moisture. "So, someone else has to be part of this. Someone who had reason to kill Kyler and would also know to create a spell similar to yours."

"I suppose," Rosemary said doubtfully. "But once more, Annie, there are extremely few people who would know how to make the sort of extraction necessary. I can only think of two or three people in the Society."

"I can check into them," Annie said insistently.

Rosemary tapped her fingers against the table. "Very well. There's Midge Mayhem—no, it's not her birth name, she changed it in the seventies—and Heather Truman, and of course, Felixa Stetter."

Annie nodded. Three suspects. That was more than she had before.

"I went to dinner with Felixa, and we had a lovely time together, so it can't be her. Midge is in a wheelchair and doesn't have the eyesight to do extractions anymore; she's over a hundred years old. Heather was at the conference, and I believe she was going on to a charity ball with the governor. It should be easy enough to check."

Annie rested her elbows against the table, staring at the rest of her uneaten sandwich. "So, according to you, none of these suspects could have done it. Are you protecting someone?"

"No, dear. I would not protect a murderer."

Annie nodded once, believing her again. The only question was, what were they overlooking? She picked up the sandwich and took a bite of it once more, chewing thoughtfully. What did it mean if nobody else in the Society could create such an extract?

"Perhaps the killer got the extract from someone," Annie mused. "Although that still leaves the spell… are you sure you destroyed it?"

Rosemary nodded. "I was ashamed for creating it in the first place. I would never have shared it."

"Who else in the Society has the means of creating new spells? It might not be yours, just one similar." Annie was hungrier, so she continued eating as her brain raced. They didn't have to look for an herbalist if the killer had bought the extraction from someone else.

Which also meant she would have something to give Adam other than Rosemary.

It made sense to Annie. If the spell was created once, it could be created again. History was full of people fighting over who was the first to create this spell or that potion. She had dabbled in various potion-making and made her own brews; she doubted she was the first to figure out how to induce visions, however.

Rosemary, however, looked doubtful. "The effects are just too similar to be a coincidence, though. Don't you think?"

"But you destroyed your spell, so it has to be a coincidence. Now. Has anyone come to you asking for the extract?"

"No, and neither have they gone to the others; the plant is carefully monitored, and even the request would have to be marked down in the Society. I can't believe that Heather, Midge, or Felixa would break the rules by not reporting it."

Annie considered this for a long moment. An idea popped into her head, and she slapped her forehead. Of course! It made complete sense! "Do you have a list of people rejected from the Society? A herbalist who could do the extraction but didn't get a place? Especially someone around the time you made that spell?"

CHAPTER FIVE

"BUT WHY WOULD any of my old classmates want to harm Kyler?" Rosemary asked. "They'd have no reason... except... oh!"

Her face went ashen, almost as pale as Monty was. Annie straightened. She had a feeling in the pit of her stomach that they had just cracked open something new in the case. Her breath caught in her throat as she waited for Rosemary to continue.

"Oh, my," Rosemary pressed her hands to her cheeks.

"What is it?" Annie urged.

"I just remembered that before I perfected the recipe for the spell, I had several drafts written in an old textbook of mine. I used magic to erase the notes because I couldn't bear to destroy the book. But if someone noticed the spells on the page, they could uncover the notes again."

Annie leaned forward. "Did you lend out this book to anyone?"

"There's a new student who is applying to be a herbalist. Her name is Ophelia Jacobson. Her mother was rejected many years ago because she wasn't very good. Ophelia is the best in her class." Rosemary's brow furrowed as she clenched her hands. "But what cause would Ophelia have to kill someone?"

"I don't know. But I have a plan to find out," Annie said.

Annie and Rosemary stayed up late, planning how they would find out if Ophelia had killed Kyler. Annie texted the name to Adam, who promised that he would investigate it. He sounded exhausted. Annie winced.

"You should get some sleep. Rosemary is hosting a Society dinner tomorrow with all this year's students, so we'll have time to learn more about Ophelia before then," she told him.

"I know. I don't like you working on this case so far away, Little Witch," Adam sighed over the phone. "Do you think I could stop by, too? Or is this a witches-only event?"

Annie sat in the room Rosemary gave her. It looked like something out of the eighties, but everything was clean and well-tended. The bed was more comfortable than it looked, too. It was big enough to hold two or three other people. She thought how nice it would be to have someone with her to sit and talk with or cuddle while watching a movie.

She felt awfully alone, even though Rosemary was in the next room.

"It's witches and witches' partners," Annie said slowly. "And I mean like fiancé and spouse sort of partner. We would have to provide evidence that you and I were together and serious about our relationship if you wanted to join."

Adam was quiet for a moment before he said, "You are my partner, though. Our relationship is serious."

"But not romantic," Annie whispered.

Her heart pounded in her chest. They had never gotten this close to talking about what was between them before. Though Annie had always found him attractive, she had tried to push aside those feelings. They had a good working relationship, and she didn't want to jeopardize that.

Adam sighed again. "No. Not romantic. So, I guess this will be up to you, Little Witch. I know you can do it. Just be careful. If this Ophelia is the person who killed Kyler, she knows who you are."

"I know. How is the cat?" Annie didn't want to stay on the harder conversation. Disappointment hit her stomach, but she masked it with a bright tone.

Adam grumbled. "I never wanted a cat, you know. I get why people like them, but I'm not a cat person. But I'm going to need more of those allergy spells. I kept sneezing while we worked at my computer today."

Annie had to stifle a giggle. "You both worked on the computer?"

"Yes. Well. He was bored and lonely. But he makes the cutest little meowing sounds when he's hungry and wants me to feed him. I got an excellent picture of him on his cat condo; I'll send it to you. I think I'm going to name him Winston."

"Oh, Adam." Annie laughed out loud. "Seems like you have a cat."

Adam made a disapproving noise in his throat. "I… guess. Update me tomorrow, okay? Goodnight, Little Witch."

"Goodnight, Adam."

Rosemary took her role as hostess seriously. Despite being up most of the night, she was at it first thing in the morning, preparing for the party. Annie was busy all day, too, and was glad that Adam could investigate Kyler's life more while she was busy setting up the sting.

It was a little unnerving to Annie that Adam wasn't with her there. But it was witch business, and even if Ophelia ended up being the murderer, it would be the Coven who would deal with this infraction.

Annie kept her expression gentle as the coven arrived. Everyone wore their best and complimented Rosemary on how wonderful everything looked. It was well into the night before Rosemary introduced Annie to Ophelia.

She was a lovely young woman with enormous eyes and red hair, currently pulled back in an elaborate system of braids and decorated with ribbons and flowers. There was a nervousness to her that Annie didn't like, though she saw no recognition in the other woman's eyes.

Rosemary greeted her with a hug. "Ophelia, I'd like you to meet one of my former students, Annie. Annie, Ophelia Jacobson is applying for the same program you were in. Perhaps you could give her some pointers?"

"I would love to," Annie said with a smile.

"Good, good. I'll leave the two of you then. Oh, there's Midge. I must go say hello." Rosemary swept off, her cotton skirt swishing around her.

Annie sipped her champagne flute of sparkling apple juice. She wanted the appearance of drinking without risking getting drunk. "So, you're applying for a herbalist apprenticeship, are you? Rosemary's the best you can learn from."

Ophelia smiled weakly. "She is, yes. I was fortunate enough to be paired with her for the exam preparation. She has learned so much that isn't in our textbooks."

"Oh, I know that! I used to find many notes and spells scribbled in the margins of the books she lent me." Annie laughed, masking her nerves.

She could talk to a murderer. Adam knew how to get people to reveal their secrets, but she wasn't sure she could do it. If Adam was here, what would he do?

"I haven't seen you around," Annie said, sipping her drink again. "Are you new to the area?"

"No, but my mother and I haven't spent much time at coven events. We moved over near Boston for a while but just moved back. She's an alchemist," Ophelia added proudly. "She almost got a spot as a herbalist, but life events made her turn down the position."

That wasn't what Rosemary had told her. Annie nodded, not giving anything away. An alchemist would have the equipment to make the poison extraction.

"What about you?" Ophelia asked. "I don't think we've met before."

"Oh, I don't live in Portland anymore. I lived in Boston for a while but moved to this cute little town a few years back. It's been wonderful." Inspiration struck Annie. There was one thing she could do to get a reaction from Ophelia if she was the killer. "I'm ready to go home, in any case. I have heard nothing from my boyfriend for a couple of days… if I'm not around, he forgets to message me."

Ophelia made a face. "Oh, I know how that is. I just recently broke up with my boyfriend… well, if you can even call a dirty cheater a boyfriend."

"He was an idiot," Annie said, lifting her glass. "You're gorgeous! He'll never get someone better than you."

"He didn't want somebody better," Ophelia said, wrinkling her nose. "He just wanted me and her and everything else."

Annie nodded sympathetically. "Greedy men are the worst. Luckily, my boyfriend's not like that. He's funny and kind; even if he isn't the most thoughtful, he's a good man. And he's great around the house."

Ophelia picked up some cookies from the buffet table. "Oh?"

It was clear she wasn't interested in this conversation, but Annie happily pretended not to notice. "Yeah. That's how we met. I hired Kyler to be my handyman and—"

"Kyler?" Ophelia snapped up straight. "Kyler North?"

Annie arched her eyebrows, surprised and excited about the reaction. Was she going to admit something? "Yes… do you know him?"

"He's the rotten ex that cheated on me! Ugh, honey, don't waste your time on that one. Dump him now, or he'll rip your heart out." Anger flared in Ophelia's eyes.

"But he seems so nice," Annie protested. "I don't believe this. He must be a different Kyler. I'm going home tomorrow, and I'm sure he'll clear up this misunderstanding."

Ophelia shook her head emphatically. "He'll do nothing but lie to you. Trust me on this one, Annie. He's nothing but trouble—"

"Ophelia!" A sharp voice snapped just behind them.

Annie jumped, her heart in her throat as she turned. A woman with greying hair pushed through the crowd toward them, leaning heavily on a cane. Her eyes widened when they landed on Annie. She recognized her.

"Mom? What's wrong?" Ophelia asked.

Mrs. Jacobson grabbed her arm, still looking with alarm at Annie. "We have to leave. I'm not feeling well."

"Hold on," Annie said, holding up a hand. "Ophelia and I are talking about Skyler North."

The blood drained from Mrs. Jacobson's face.

CHAPTER SIX

ANNIE DREW herself up straight as the fear flooded Mrs. Jacobson's face. Triumph rushed through her. She had cracked the case! It was clear from the expression on this woman's face that she knew something... and judging by the confusion Ophelia was showing, it would not be an accessory to murder.

"I don't think you need to bring up that man," Mrs. Jacobson stuttered.

Ophelia shook her head. "But I had to. He's dating Annie now, and I wanted to warn her of him. The silence you've had from him the last couple of days? Get used to it. He never texts first, and half the time when you text him, he won't reply."

Annie shook her head. The poor girl had no idea, did she? "Ophelia told me you are an alchemist, Mrs. Jacobson. That must mean you're very used to delicate procedures... and trained as a herbalist. So, you would know how to make plant extractions."

Rosemary joined them, her aged face stern.

"I don't need to answer anything you ask me," Mrs. Jacobson said rather rudely. "I know all about *you*. You're misusing your talents, wasting them on non-witches, using them to work with the cops. If you're interested in crime and order, you ought to join the witch peace-keepers."

"I'm afraid you have to answer our questions," Rosemary said, her voice growing sharp.

Annie smiled, grateful for her mentor's backup. "You see, I am working in an official capacity at the time being. Kyler North was murdered with a witch's spell, and then the murder was covered by a secondary spell that nearly cursed me."

Ophelia gasped, covering her mouth. "Kyler's dead?"

"He is." Annie's eyes never left Mrs. Jacobson.

"Tell me, when did you decide to kill Kyler, Mrs. Jacobson?" Rosemary asked, her voice even. "Was it after you learned he cheated on your daughter and broke her heart, or was it before? I believe you are against witches dating non-witches, after all."

Mrs. Jacobson spluttered. "I don't know what you're talking about!"

Annie shook her head, unable to stop herself from smiling. "Wrong, and we can prove it, Mrs. Jacobson. The Society will give the human police permission to test your alchemy set. I'm sure the toxins from *Strychnos toxifera* will be found still."

"The extractions are notoriously difficult to clean off," Rosemary added.

"I'm not an herbalist. The Society made sure of that."

Rosemary frowned. "You failed the trials. Regrettably, your passion wasn't where you excelled, but I daresay you have found a work-around for that, haven't you? I would never have thought of extracting the essence from plants through alchemy. If only... you could have revolutionized our understanding of the discipline."

Mrs. Jacobson's hands clenched. "Could have, you say?"

"Could have," Rosemary repeated. "But now all you will be known for is killing that man. I can't find it in myself to blame you, not really. By all accounts, he was terrible for your daughter. But she had already left him. Why kill him now?"

"Mom?" Ophelia drew back from her, eyes wide. "Mom, you didn't—"

"Quiet," Mrs. Jacobson snapped. "Just keep quiet, Ophelia. They don't have any proof... all they're doing is making fools of themselves in front of the Society."

"Are we, though?" Annie asked.

Throughout the conversation, more and more people had turned to look at the four of them as they argued. The expressions ranged from doubtful to confused to outright hostile. But the Society was slowly gathering behind Annie and Rosemary, showing their support silently.

"This is a witches' matter," Annie said, projecting her voice so all could hear. "We don't want to involve the non-witch police unless there is cause. Ophelia."

Stepping around Mrs. Jacobson, Annie turned her gaze to Ophelia. She looked utterly horrified; it was easy enough to fake the expressions like she was doing, but not the pallor of her skin or the sheer emotion in her eyes. Annie felt a rush of sympathy for her.

It couldn't be easy to know that your mother killed your ex-boyfriend. The question of why still lingered, though. Was it just revenge for breaking Ophelia's heart?

Ophelia turned her head first as though she didn't want to answer Annie's question. But then she slowly lifted her chin and met Annie's gaze.

"Do you know a reason your mother would want to kill Kyler North?" Annie asked. She tried to mimic Adam's calm tones.

"Say nothing," Mrs. Jacobson hissed.

Ophelia ignored her. "I can do more than that. I can tell you she did it. She had me use her alchemy set to extract some plant materials. I thought it was odd, but she told me it was to help manage the Pine Beetle infestations up in Canada."

Mutters broke out in the watching crowd.

"Ophelia!" Mrs. Jacobson glared at her.

"Why did she kill Kyler?" Annie asked.

The young woman swallowed visibly. She glanced around as though looking for someone to answer her. She looked so young and vulnerable that Annie couldn't help but feel bad. Now she realized this should have been a more private discussion. It was too late for that, however.

Taking a deep breath, Ophelia squared her shoulders. "Because I'm pregnant, and Kyler is the father."

The surrounding muttering grew even louder. Tears spilled over Ophelia's cheeks.

"I'm pregnant," she said again. "And my mother was furious that I had let myself get pregnant by a non-witch. I kept the baby. I plan to raise my child myself, and when I told Kyler, he said he would support me. He didn't want to be together but would stay in our lives and agree to child support."

Annie put an arm around Ophelia. "And so, you would be forever bound to him."

Ophelia buried her face in Annie's shoulder and cried.

Rosemary faced Mrs. Jacobson. "Are you going to deny the testimony of your daughter, or will you admit your guilt?"

"I... I... I did it to protect her. He was a terrible man! He would destroy her if he had a presence in her life. You didn't see how he treated her... the way she lost her spark while she was with him. And to carry that monster's baby?"

"My baby," Ophelia cried. "It's *my* baby!"

Anne transferred Ophelia to Rosemary's comforting embrace and faced Mrs. Jacobson. In the past, it had always been Adam that did this. She straightened her shoulders, her victory tainted by the grief of the situation.

"Mrs. Jacobson, I will have to place you under witch's arrest. Please do not resist."

"I won't resist." Mrs. Jacobson let out a ragged breath as she sagged into a nearby chair. She held up the cane and pulled it in two, revealing a hidden sword. This is the weapon I enchanted to kill him."

Annie carefully took the weapon. There would no doubt be trace evidence left on it.

"I left that bad luck curse in his apartment when I moved his body there, hoping it would prevent the police from figuring it out. And I made sure that that paralytic spell would hit you because I knew you would be the only person there to stop my plan from working." Mrs. Jacobson lowered her head. "Goddess help me; I just wanted to protect my baby girl."

Winston, the cat, bounced around the living room, chasing the feathered cat toy Monty played with. Annie was right that Monty was taken by the cat, and Winston would stay in her house when Adam was working. Still, Adam had gotten used to having Winston around —and since Winston was already so bonded to him, he didn't want to traumatize the little guy further.

Annie still found it funny how quickly Adam had adopted the cat, but she also found it incredibly sweet. She didn't need yet another reason to be attracted to him.

The man himself stretched his legs out in front of him, hands clasped over his toned stomach. Annie had just finished describing what happened at the Society dinner, and Adam kept grinning the whole time.

"Next time, I'll be there to see you in action myself," he said.

Annie rolled her eyes. "I doubt there will be a next time. I found I don't enjoy investigating on my own. I like working with you."

"And I enjoy working with you, Little Witch," Adam replied. "I didn't like having such a separate investigation, either."

"You were worried about me," Annie accused playfully.

"Worried?" Adam shook his head.

Annie felt her stomach drop a little. "You weren't worried?"

"Of course not. I know you can handle yourself. Well, maybe a little worried," Adam admitted sheepishly. "But I knew you would solve the case. What is going to happen to Ophelia and her mother now?"

"We will investigate Ophelia to ensure she didn't know about her mother's plot. If she's found innocent, which I believe she will be, she will be given compensation for her troubles and continue living her life." Annie snickered as Winston pounced on the feather and started a tug-of-war with Monty. "As for her mother, she'll be going to jail. This is strictly forbidden."

"I'm glad it's resolved. And I'm proud of you, Annie. You found the killer in less than two days. That's an impressive record." He took her hand in his, squeezing.

Warmth spread through Annie from that touch. As she stared into his eyes, the words she longed to say bubbled up her throat. "I love—" No, she couldn't admit the depth of her feelings, not yet! "Working with you."

Was that disappointment in Adam's eyes? If it was, it was gone quickly. He smiled. "I love working with you as well. I hope we have many more cases in front of us."

The End

AN ANNIE ARCHER PARANORMAL MYSTERY

THE CASE OF THE

AMETHYST PENDANT

A COZY MYSTERY

DAISY LANDISH

PROLOGUE

WINSTON, the cat, lay stretched on the old rug in *Annie Archer's Antiques and Artifacts*. His tail flicked back and forth as he watched the ghost attempt to rummage through the fresh boxes of antiques Annie had just got in. If they were lucky, they'd find something they could take home.

The ghost grinned when he found an old typewriter. Perfect! He couldn't interact with much of the 'living' world, not since his rather tragic death a few decades ago. Fortunately, Annie wasn't just some regular live person who couldn't see or interact with Monty. She was a witch and could cast spells on things to make it easier for him to entertain himself.

"Monty, what are you doing?" Annie asked sharply from behind him.

The ghost glared over his shoulder. He pointed at the typewriter and then himself. This was his typewriter now. It was the least she could do after she moved into his house and started calling him 'Monty.' Although Monty was as good of a name as anything else... it wasn't like he remembered what he'd been called during his life.

Annie glanced at the typewriter. "Do you have a book you want to write?"

Monty huffed silently. That was about being dead and his ghostly form having a slash across his throat. He couldn't make noise at all, even if, logically, he should be able to. He signed instead.

"Yes."

"Oh." Annie looked mildly impressed. "What about?"

"My life history, of course."

Annie pulled the typewriter from the box and checked it over. "It looks like it's in good working order. I'll get some extra supplies for you as soon as I can. For now..."

She dug into her pocket and pulled out a little vial of sparkling green powder. She sprinkled the powder over the typewriter, and it clicked and whirled as though it was one of those modern machines.

It stopped soon enough, and Monty took a seat before it, testing it out. The buttons clicked and stamped the paper in it.

This is the story of which I have longed to tell, he wrote happily.

A brass-bell tinkling made him look up. Detective Adam Parker strode into the store wearing his usual suit. Monty scowled at the detective. In his day, courting couples were never alone together, yet this detective found it prudent to make every attempt to be alone with Annie.

Since Annie had nobody else in this town, it was up to Monty to defend her against this man. He narrowed his eyes at the detective, though he knew Adam couldn't see him.

I'm watching you; he typed quickly as Adam and Annie greeted one another. He yanked the paper from the typewriter and carried it over to Adam. Monty shrugged off and Winston perked up.

The next moment, Winston was battling the paper while Annie and Adam laughed, watching him. Monty tried to shoo the cat away; this was important!

"Thanks for watching Winston while I was out of town," Adam said. He helped Annie sort out her new donations.

Winston yanked the paper from Monty's hands and tore it into pieces.

Monty gave up and returned to his typewriter. There was time to warn Adam Parker later. As he typed once more, Annie gasped.

His head shot up, a silent snarl on his lips. But rather than Adam getting handsy as he'd expected, he saw Annie pull a necklace from the box. Her eyes were wide as she inspected it.

"Is that the Rizzoli necklace?" Adam asked.

"No. No," Annie said, firmer the second time as she turned the necklace over in her hands. "Gosh. I thought it was for a second there. But look, this is all costume jewelry. Glass and painted tin."

Adam leaned over to inspect the necklace. "I haven't thought about the Rizzoli case for years."

"Our first case together," Annie murmured. "That was just after I'd finalized my divorce from William."

Monty blocked them out as he typed.

CHAPTER ONE

LEAVING behind Boston was the hardest thing Annie Archer had ever done. She had thought divorcing William would be the hardest, but it wasn't. Her relationship with William had been over for some time before either had the guts to admit it. It was clear that most of what kept Annie in Boston was linked to William.

Quitting her job and heading to a small town with nothing but her savings to rely on would have, at one time, been unthinkable. As it was, she had still cried for hours after finally deciding.

She knew it was the right thing to do. But it was still tricky.

Turtle Bay was the perfect place to start over. She already had an interview at a security place and a few lines on properties in the area. She'd be renting, but hopefully, she would soon find a lovely little house on which to pay down.

When her GPS told her she had arrived at her destination, Annie turned off the car. She stared at the magnificent house as she got out. It was built in an Edwardian style, with dark red brick, sharp gables, and white wooden trim. A small, round balcony curved from one of the upper bedrooms, sitting over the ground-level, wraparound porch. Flowers grew around the edge of the porch, and the door had a large stained-glass window in it.

The said door opened, and Annie jumped slightly. She half-expected a ghost of the past to drift from the house, but it was a woman of flesh and blood.

A short, squat woman with curly grey hair squinted at her. "Annie Archer?"

"That's me," Annie grabbed her suitcase from the backseat of her car. "Are you Nikki Rizzoli?"

"Of course," Nikki said with a laugh. "Come on in, my dear. I've gotten your room ready for you. I hope you like turquoise."

"I do, thank you," Annie replied politely.

Nikki held the door open for her, casting an appraising look at the suitcase. "Is that all you've brought with you, dear?"

"For now. I've put the rest of my belongings in storage," Annie said.

"Ah. Of course. Now, the kitchen is through there; you'll find the mudroom and laundry on the other side. Over here," Nikki pointed at a door on the opposite side of the narrow corridor, "is the parlor. I'll give you more of a tour once you're settled in. The stairs upstairs are down here."

"Thank you," Annie replied. She admired the trim and wallpaper as she followed Nikki. "This is a beautiful house. You've kept the historic charm intact. It's even more lovely than the pictures the rental agent showed me."

Nikki beamed. "Thank you, my dear. My father built this house. I was born in the same room I keep for myself now."

"Oh." Annie wasn't entirely sure how to respond to that.

They were soon in Annie's new room. The walls were papered in turquoise flowers, with a hand-braided rug of the same color. The bedspread again was turquoise on the canopy bed. Lacy white curtains hung around it. The room also had a reading chair, an empty book-shelf, and a fireplace.

The hearth clearly was the original brick, but an electric fireplace was now occupying the space. Annie tamped down on her disappointment. It was probably for the best. She couldn't imagine having to keep this room clean from wood smoke.

"Are the beds original, too?" she asked Nikki as she put her suitcase next to the chair.

"Oh, no. I had those made special to look authentic… But I always found the real ones to be just a little too creaky. I get enough of that from these old bones," Nikki laughed.

"You have a walk-in closet connected to your own bathroom," Nikki continued. She walked to a relatively small door next to the bed and opened it up to reveal another, smaller room.

Annie followed her through, her eyes lighting up as she walked into the closet. It was bigger than any closet she had had before. There would be lots of room to store her clothes and a few boxes of her belongings. She might even downsize her storage container and save some money on that.

"My father originally built these three rooms all as bedrooms," Nikki said as she led Annie on through a second door. "When I converted it into a rental unit, I renovated it. You know, that closet was a full room on its own? It was where Father had the nanny sleep. But then these old buildings usually have cramped quarters."

They entered the ensuite bathroom. Annie gaped. She hadn't seen pictures of the room she'd be staying in and was amazed at what she saw.

The bathroom was tiled in white, with a Roman-style mosaic all on the wall closest to the house's interior. A vast, double-headed shower stood along one wall, next to a sink with enough counter space. Annie thought she could set up a little kitchenette here. The claw-foot bathtub sat precisely in the middle of the room.

French doors led to the balcony, framed by privacy curtains.

"Oh, my," Annie exclaimed, clapping her hands. "This is far more than I expected. Are you sure about the rent? The apartment my husband… *ex-husband* and I shared was the same size and half as fancy, and we paid at least twice as much for it."

Nikki waved her hand with a 'pssh' noise. "Of course, I'm sure about rent. I don't need the money, my dear. What I do with my house here is set up for witching finding their feet again. Please think of me like a bonus grandmother. So long as you apply yourself in Turtle Bay, you'll find that you are quite successful here."

Annie impulsively hugged the older woman. "Thank you."

"Of course," Nikki patted her back. "Don't think this is all for nothing, though. I expect you will do great things with this opportunity. Set yourself up to rebuild your future now."

Annie nodded once as she released Nikki. William had expressed no distaste for her magic. But there had always seemed to be some tension between them about her being a witch. Annie had tried to get him to talk to her about it, but he never would.

But she didn't have to spare these thoughts for William now. The divorce had completed over three months ago. Sure, William was already engaged to another woman.

Annie sighed. She knew William hadn't cheated on her. She also knew that they hadn't been good together. They had stopped communicating and sharing their struggles, hopes, and dreams. From the outside, their relationship had been perfect. Both worked, both kept house, they had no major problems...

Except one. And that was that they had no spark.

So much so that she couldn't even be angry at him for moving on so quickly after the divorce. If anything, she felt sorry for herself. William was a good guy, in any case. He'd told her about his growing feelings for his coworker before he had done anything about those feelings.

The thing she would always be grateful to him for was his honesty.

"Thank you," she said to Nikki, gently pulling her mind away from William. "I hope you'll let me help around the house, at least."

Nikki made another 'pssh' noise. "Focus on finding your feet. You can use the kitchen if you like, but I'm rather particular about how things are cleaned. You're responsible for your room, and that is all."

"Thank you," Annie said again.

"I'll let you get settled in," Nikki said.

She left through the closet and bedroom.

Annie opened the French doors and stepped onto the balcony. It was odd to have a balcony off the bathroom, but she could picture herself standing here, looking out over the town. Nikki's house stood on a hill with a view over Turtle Bay. The bay itself sparkled blue in the distance—quite a lovely sight.

Annie smiled to herself, and she leaned against the balcony railing. This was perfect for a new place to start over. A new job, a new living situation, new friends. Everything was going to be just perfect.

And she had Nikki Rizzoli to thank for giving her such an opportunity.

Grinning, Annie went back to her room to unpack. While putting her clothes in the closet, she noticed a small box sitting on the shelf's corner. Curious, she picked it up and went back to her room. Had Nikki left it in her room by mistake, or was it a gift?

She opened the box and gasped.

CHAPTER TWO

THE NECKLACE NESTLED inside the ordinary box was exquisite. Annie had always been interested in antiques and vintage items and knew instantly that this wasn't any replication. A fist-sized amethyst sat in a heavy gold setting. Several smaller gems were arranged on either side of the big amethyst. The setting was obviously old; at first glance, Annie estimated it was something from the 1700s.

Such a beautiful piece hardly seemed to be something a person as meticulous as Nikki Rizzoli would overlook. Was there another reason it was in the room?

Annie lifted it carefully from where it was nestled in worn velvet. It was the typical ornate metalwork of the Georgian era, the amethysts cut with expert precision. She couldn't help but take it to the bathroom and stand in front of the mirror, looking to see how it would be around her neck.

"Not really my style," Annie decided as she lowered it again. "Not that it's mine at all."

Maybe it was a replica. Annie had some training in recognizing jewelry and antiques, but at this point, it was nothing more than a hobby. One day she hoped to know enough to open up her own antique shop.

She turned the necklace over in her hands and caught sight of an etching on the back of it. She peered closer, turning the chain this way and that to see what it said. The letters had almost been polished right off, but she finally found the right angle. *Maggie, 1755-1753. Lacey, 1732-1202.*

"Strange," she murmured.

How could the end dates be before the start dates? It made little sense.

She turned it back over, and sunlight glinted off the cut face of the amethyst. The gem glowed internally as though being charged by the light. A subtle buzzing feeling flowed through Annie's fingers. She gasped again and dropped it back into the velvet box.

Whatever this necklace was, it was magical.

Swallowing hard, Annie quickly shut the box and carried it back to her room, where she had left it on the bookcase. The buzzing stopped, and she wiped her hands against her jeans, swallowing hard. She wanted to open the box again but forced herself to continue putting away her things.

Once the single suitcase was taken care of, Annie carefully wrapped the box in a shawl and carried it out to find Nikki.

The older witch was in the parlor, dusting. She smiled when she saw Annie. "Settled in already?"

"Pretty much," Annie agreed. "But I found this necklace in my room. It's got a magical aura, and I'm sure you didn't mean to leave it there."

"A necklace?" Nikki repeated. Her brow furrowed as she tucked her dust rag into her waistband and hurried over.

Annie carefully unwrapped the box and opened it. Nikki's face became stricken when she looked at it. "Oh. Oh, dear."

"What is it?" Annie asked, as curious about Nikki's reaction as the necklace itself. "Is it dangerous?"

Nikki reverently took the necklace from the box. "Not at all, child. This necklace has been passed from parent to child for generations through my family. It shows the names of the current holder on the back."

"It bears the names Maggie and Lacey," Annie said. "As well as dates from the Georgian era."

Nikki turned it over in her hands, chuckling slightly. "Those aren't dates, my dear. They're times. It shows the time in a twenty-four-hour clock the heir took their first breath and when they will take their last. For instance, mine was 100-2359. Hardly dates now, are they?"

"Oh. That makes a lot more sense than end dates that come after start dates," Annie said.

"I'll just put this in the safe." Nikki hurried over to a large oil painting hanging above the parlor's fireplace. It swung open, and Annie turned her face away respectfully as Nikki opened the safe behind it.

Nikki closed the safe and put the painting back in place, then wiped her hands off. "Let me show you the kitchen. You're free to use any magical ingredients I have there, but I should show you how I have everything organized."

She hurried out of the room, hoping to make Annie forget what she had just put in the wall safe. Annie followed, still curious about it. If Maggie and Lacey, whoever they were, should have the necklace, why did Nikki have it?

When she entered the kitchen, though, those thoughts left her. She had imagined a cramped little kitchen filled to the brim with many antique baking pans.

Instead, she stepped into the dream kitchen of any professional chef and baker. Large ovens stood stacked on one side of the room, a grill beside them, and a stovetop with elements next to that. One entire wall was cupboards labeled with everything from *baking supplies* to *spices for sleep*.

Not only that, but Nikki had a walk-in refrigerator and freezer both. A three-piece sink sat under a massive window. It was a fantastic place, and Annie was already excited about using these facilities.

"This is amazing," she exclaimed as she paced through the open space. "I wouldn't have thought you would have enough room for this."

"I may have a few space-enlargement spells in the corners," Nikki said with a cheeky grin. "I do enough cooking and baking that I want space to work. And no matter how much I love the old way of doing things, you can't convince me to use anything but the latest cooking gear."

Annie opened one cupboard labeled *Potion Ingredients*. Everything she could think of needing was in there. "Oh, wow. Do you grow these herbs yourself?"

"No, there's an apothecary in town where you'll find supplies," Nikki replied. "But people around here know me as the friendly witch and often come to me for minor spells to help them. I admit I'm not great at potions, though."

"I see. Well, I'll have to help you fill your orders. My mentor, Rosemary, says I'm very proficient with potions."

Annie grinned at her, forgetting all about the amethyst necklace.

"Maybe you would like to help me prepare some, then?" Nikki asked pleasantly. "I need a few sleeping potions made for Mr. Henderson down the way… he's a cantankerous old man, but when he gets some decent sleep, he can be quite sweet, actually."

"We had best give him something to be sweet about, then!" Annie said gallantly.

They spent the rest of the day chatting animatedly while they cooked and baked together. Annie relished in the conversation. She had always enjoyed the act of communal cooking and hadn't been able to take part for some time.

When evening rolled around, Nikki prepared a roast chicken with blood orange sauce. Annie had never tried blood oranges before and was nervous about it.

"It's not actual blood," Nikki laughed when Annie expressed her doubts. "See? It's just been bred for the fruit to be a delicious, dark red. You'll adore it, I promise. Now, the dishes are in that cupboard," Nikki pointed, "be a dear and set the table, will you?"

Annie nodded. She gathered the dishes she needed and took them through the swinging door into the dining room. The room was carpeted in forest green, with sea-green walls and a singular lamp hanging from the ceiling. The shade was shaped like a turtle, stained with many bright colors.

Soon enough, Nikki brought two plates out with the chicken steaming on a pile of fluffy white rice paired with fragrant asparagus.

"This looks delicious," Annie said as she took her spot. "Thank you so much for this."

"It's no problem at all, my dear," Nikki said.

Annie was still a little nervous about the blood orange sauce. It was a deep red, almost the color of blood. The scent was sweet and floral, almost, though. Her eyes widened when she stirred a bit of the sauce into the rice and tasted it. It was sweet and tart all at once, tasting like flowers were budding on her tongue and raining nectar onto her tastebuds.

It was so good that she had to take a bite of the sauce with the chicken. She closed her eyes as she savored the taste.

Nikki chuckled. "I take it you like it?"

"Very much so," Annie agreed.

They didn't talk much while they dined. If Annie hadn't been so caught up in the new bold flavors she was experiencing for the first time, she might have noticed something off about her new landlady.

As it was, she noticed nothing off. Even when she found her eyelids too heavy to keep open at eight o'clock, she only thought the day's events made her so tired.

If only she paid more attention...

CHAPTER THREE

KNOCKING WOKE HER.

Annie squeezed her eyes shut more, trying to tell herself that the sound came from her dream. Her mind was muddled, but she felt cozy in this soft, warm bed.

More knocking.

She groaned as she cracked her eyes open. Bleary-eyed, she saw the clock read five o'clock. She bolted upright, first sure she had slept the day away. But as she realized where she was, she realized the faint light outside was from streetlamps. Five in the morning, then.

"Nikki?" she called as she grabbed her robe.

The knocking paused, and then a gruff male voice spoke. "I'm afraid not. I'm Detective Adam Parker of the Turtle Bay police department—I need to speak with you."

What was a police officer doing here?

Annie threw on her fuzzy bathrobe and grabbed a small potion from her nightstand; if the man on the other side of the door was lying, she could throw this in his face and escape. But the door wasn't locked. So, if he *was* lying, why wouldn't he have snuck into the room and robbed her while she slept?

Where was Nikki?

Annie turned on her lights and opened the door, holding the potion ready to throw it. The man on the other side had already stepped back, a badge in his hand. All the lights in the house were on, illuminating his grim expression. If not for that look, his face would be rather handsome.

"Here is my identification," the man said, holding his other hand.

Annie glanced at it, then yawned. The identification stated this was Detective Adam Parker, all right. She needed to keep her guard up... but she leaned against the doorframe, exhaustion pulling at her. Her hand drooped.

"What are you here for?" she asked, her brow furrowed. "Where's Nikki?"

"You're Annie Tremlett, correct?" Detective Parker asked, his tone clipped.

"It's Annie Archer now," she said, straightening. "I changed my name back after my divorce. What is this about?"

Detective Parker frowned at her. "We received a call reporting that there was something strange happening in this house. Did you hear anything last night?"

Annie blinked at him, a cold sort of feeling in her stomach. "I went to bed right after supper, around eight. And I—" she yawned, her eyes shutting of their own accord. Her head drooped, and she would have fallen over if Adam hadn't caught her. "—I've been asleep since."

"Geoff, get the paramedics up here. I think she's been drugged."

Drugged? Why would anyone drug her? Adam helped her to the chair, set her down in it, and then retrieved a blanket to spread over her. A tenderness to his concern pleased Annie, even though she knew it shouldn't.

"I see you signed tenancy papers for Mrs. Rizzoli's room," Adam continued as he crouched next to her. "How long have you been renting this room?"

"Moved in yesterday."

Adam frowned. "Just yesterday?"

"Yes." Annie felt the detective needed more information than that, so she sighed heavily. "You see, I divorced my husband recently and decided I needed a fresh start. Nikki rents to witches, and I thought this seemed like a lovely little place to start fresh."

A young woman dressed in a paramedic uniform came into the room. She took Annie's vitals and drew a small vial of blood. Annie watched her with detached disinterest.

"If you're done, I'm exhausted," she said, trying to be polite. "Whatever this is about can wait until tomorrow. I'm surprised Nikki let you in so early in the morning, anyway. What's this all about? You said you got a call… a call about what?"

Adam seemed to deliberate about something. He glanced at the paramedic, who was checking Annie's head now.

Annie still felt so tired… unnaturally tired. She struggled to focus on the detective's face. But as it turned out, the fight was too intense for her. She didn't even hear what he said as she fell, hard, into another deep sleep.

Detective Adam Parker caught Annie Archer as she slumped once more. Her head landed on his shoulder, and she released a soft snore. His lips tightened as he glanced at the paramedic.

"We should get her to a hospital," the paramedic said, looking worried. "I don't think she even realized she was answering my questions. Definitely drugged."

"The question remains whether it was by magic or non-magic means," Adam said.

He picked up the slight woman and carried her back to the bed, laying her down gently. With the paramedic lingering nearby, he lifted his two-way radio and ordered a stretcher to be brought up.

He knew she might have drugged herself to eliminate herself as a suspect. He hoped not. She had kind eyes and looked like the sort of person who would make Turtle Bay a better place.

There's no place for sentimentality in crime, he told himself as a couple more paramedics came into the room with a stretcher. *Appearances mean very little.*

There was no 'waking up' the second time. One moment Annie was dead asleep, the next, wide awake. She sat up, humming, and had already swung her legs off the bed before she realized she was in a hospital room.

Her eyes widened, and her jaw dropped. "What?"

A knock came on the door, reminding her of last night. She shivered as she slid back on the bed, pulling the blankets up to her chest. She had been changed from her nightgown into a hospital nightgown. Even though she knew the nurses and doctors would have been professional about it, she still blushed.

The door opened and in stepped a familiar man. It took Annie only half a second to place him. "Detective Parker."

"Miss Archer. Or do you prefer—"

"Miss Archer is fine." Annie chewed her lip, that icy feeling back. "What happened last night?"

Adam came further into the room, leaving the door open slightly. "I'm sorry to tell you this, but Mrs. Nicole Rizzoli was murdered last night. The coroner puts her death at around midnight."

"11:59," Annie whispered. "When she drew her last breath."

Adam arched a brow as he pulled a notebook out of his jacket. "Are you a visionary witch, Miss Archer?"

"No. No, it's something she told me yesterday when I found the necklace." Annie touched her collarbone as though she could feel the heaviness of the gold and amethysts. Her brow furrowed. "The wall safe. Was she robbed?"

"We have found nothing amiss. What were you saying about a necklace?"

How could he be so cold about this? Annie took a shuddering breath. "I found this necklace in my room while I put my things away. She told me that the names on it reflected its current owners, as well as the times in the day they took their first breath... and when they'd take their last," she added.

Adam stared at her as though he couldn't quite believe her.

"Nikki put it in her wall safe. The names on the back were Maggie and Lacey. It has to be connected somehow." *Nikki had been so disturbed to see it.*

Adam made a note in his book. "How long have you known the victim?"

"Nikki," Annie snapped, dropping her hand. "Her name was Nikki."

Adam's gaze softened. "Miss Archer, I understand this is a difficult situation. It helps the investigation not to let my feelings get in the way. I knew Nikki, too. It's easier for me to look at the case objectively if I compartmentalize it. I apologize if that makes it more difficult for you, but it's the way I need to approach this case."

Annie sighed. It was an appropriate answer. "We had exchanged some emails and did a handful of video calls. Otherwise, I met her yesterday."

"The doctors report you had a sleeping potion in your system," Adam continued, his voice flat again. "Did you take the potion yourself?"

"No. Some chicken and blood orange sauce should be left in the fridge; you should test that." Annie squinted at the ceiling. "But I don't understand why Nikki would drug me."

"You think...?" Adam stared at her questioningly.

Annie considered the events and explained slowly. She had been helping Nikki make sleeping potions before Nikki made supper. There wasn't any possibility of accidental cross-contamination, nor any chance that someone else could have drugged the food. Nikki never left the kitchen.

"Which can only mean that Nikki herself drugged me," Annie concluded. "But why? I know this has something to do with that necklace, Detective. We must get back to the house and check the wall safe."

"I don't—" Adam started.

Annie swung off the bed, holding the blankets to her body. "How was she killed? And where are my clothes?"

Adam picked up a bag from the floor and put it on the bed. "She was strangled. The bruising pattern indicates some sort of chain was used."

The necklace. Annie had heard of magical artifacts being imbued with dangerous energies. She felt that this necklace was one of them... and with a fresh chill, she was extra grateful she hadn't given into the temptation of trying it on the previous day.

CHAPTER FOUR

ADAM FOLLOWED Annie as she hesitated at the entrance to the parlor where Nikki had been killed. Regardless of what he said about compartmentalization, this case hit him hard. He might not have known Nikki too well, but she always greeted him with a friendly smile whenever they passed each other on the streets.

Nothing in Annie's countenance showed that she was guilty of this crime, and for that, Adam was grateful. He had to trust his gut in a lot of things, but usually, he didn't trust it for suspects. Yes, he was an excellent judge of character, but he had also learned that crimes were often committed by the people you'd least expect.

Everything in his instincts said Annie was trustworthy, however. And he had to believe that... for now, at least.

Annie finally straightened her shoulders and marched into the room. Her eyes moved to a chair across from the TV, shivering. Adam made a mental note of that; she assumed Nikki had been in the chair when she died, but they had found her body lying near the entrance as though she had been trying to escape her attacker.

"So where is this safe?" Adam asked her.

Annie grabbed the edge of the large oil painting hanging above the mantle and pulled it out. It swung open to reveal a metal safe behind it.

"I checked behind that painting, and there was nothing there," Adam protested.

"It's magic," Annie explained. She tilted her head this way and that as she peered at the lock. "It's been spelled so that only other people with magic can open it. This is safe, however... I didn't see what combination she used."

Adam joined her, inspecting the safe. He reached out and tried the door; it swung open easily. The interior chamber was packed with documents and cash.

"The necklace is gone," Annie murmured.

"Why would they take a necklace but leave these here?" Adam snapped latex gloves onto his hands and selected a packet of documents. He whistled. "These are bonds. If I'm correct, there's got to be at least a million dollars here."

Annie stepped back from the safe, putting her arms around her middle. "That's proof, then. They weren't after money. They were after the necklace."

Adam put the bonds back and pulled out his phone; after requesting the forensics team be sent ASAP, he took Annie by the elbow and led her back into the hall. She was shaking like a leaf, tears glinting in her eyes.

"Are you sure she said nothing? You didn't hear anything?"

Annie shook her head. "I don't understand what happened. Why would she drug me? It doesn't make any sense."

"You know what else makes little sense?" Adam asked dryly. "Leaving all those valuables in the safe and taking one necklace. Why would the killer only be interested in a single piece of jewelry?"

Annie rubbed her forehead, a heavy frown on her face. She was thinking hard, and Adam found he liked the way her lips puckered while she did so.

"The necklace was magic," she finally said, looking up. "Nikki told me the names on the back were the current owners. Maggie and Lacey. It was passed down through the generations, and she seemed surprised to see it. It's possible that nobody took the necklace, that it simply moved to whom it was supposed to go next."

"Or maybe the thief wanted to use the magic in it," Adam said.

Annie nodded slowly. "That's possible, too. But I believe that Maggie and Lacey are the people the necklace was passed to. Did Nikki have daughters?"

"No daughters. One son, but nobody's seen him for ages. From what I understand, he and Nikki had a serious falling out fifteen years ago."

Annie's gaze was empty as she met his eyes. "Then he has to be a suspect, right? As Nikki's son, he gets everything else except for the necklace. Why should he take the money when he inherits it anyway?"

"On the other hand, by leaving it behind, he's making himself a prime suspect for that specific reason," Adam pointed out.

She smirked at him, a glimmer in her eyes. "Then I guess it just depends on how intelligent he is."

By this time, the forensics team had arrived. Adam asked Annie to wait on the porch while he took care of things; once he had the team set to work, he went back out to her and invited her to walk with him along the street. It was the best part of town, with well-maintained character homes and beautifully maintained yards.

"I have another theory for you to chew on," Adam said as they walked down the sidewalk. "Nikki accidentally mixed a sleeping potion into the sauce. It wasn't meant for you but a result of careless-ness on her part. You go to bed, and she goes to the parlor. At some point, she retrieves the necklace and puts it on."

Annie opened her mouth, looking like she was going to argue.

"Allow me to finish," Adam held up a hand.

Annie huffed but nodded.

"She puts it on but doesn't shut the safe all the way. She falls asleep, only to be awoken sometime later by an intruder. The thief sees the necklace and demands it; Nikki refuses because it's a family heirloom. Since she is still under the potion's effects, she tries to run. The thief yanks the necklace off her, strangling her in the process."

Annie stopped and looked at him with realization in her eyes. "And the thief takes nothing in the safe because, even though it hasn't been locked, they can't find it because they don't have magic."

"It's possible now, isn't it?"

"It is." Annie wandered to a bench and slumped into it. She rested her elbows on her knees and her chin in her hands. "Well. I guess this isn't as clear-cut as I thought it was. I wish I knew something that would help us figure it out."

Adam couldn't stop an amused smile. "Us?"

Annie looked up at him, opening her mouth. She stopped herself, and her cheeks turned a pale pink as she ducked her head again. "Uh, I mean you."

"It's quite all right. The police force here in Turtle Bay is small," Adam said.

He sat next to her, breathing the summer floral scents deeply. He loved this place; it was his reason for staying there, despite knowing he would never get any acclaim in it. His mood turned melancholy.

"When I was a young boy, I wished I was magical. It seemed like such a blessing. These days, though, I can see how witches are hounded for impossible cures at every turn, if not outright being told they shouldn't exist." He shook his head, remembering the protestors setting up outside the apothecary when it first opened. "I thought things had gotten better. I very much hope this murder had nothing to do with Nikki being a witch."

"If it was, don't you think they would have killed me, too?" Annie asked pointedly. "I'm a witch; I moved in, and everyone knows that Nikki only rents to witches. She was killed at midnight, but you weren't called until closer to five in the morning. I was in bed, sleeping, that whole time. They had plenty of time to come after me."

"That's true."

Annie leaned closer to him, bumping his shoulder with hers. "So the prime suspects are Nikki's son, Maggie, Lacey, or an unknown thief party."

"It's a comprehensive list," Adam teased. "Except we don't know who Maggie and Lacey are. We have no clues except the times they took their first breath and when they are supposed to take their last breaths. It's not much to go on."

Annie smirked at him. "Maybe not for you. But I happen to be a witch, and I know I can track them down based on that information alone. So, while I find them, you can interrogate Nikki's son, and when we reconvene, we can share notes."

Adam wanted to laugh. He would have loved to make a deal with this witch and her sparkling eyes. He had investigated many cases over the course of his career, and nobody close to the case was ever this interested in helping him to solve it.

"I don't think that's wise," he said reluctantly.

"Why—oh." Annie's face fell. "I see… it's because I left a suspect off my list."

Adam's brows furrowed together. "What do you mean?"

Annie let out a heavy breath, looking toward the distant bay. "Me."

CHAPTER FIVE

SINCE ANNIE HAD WORKED in security for many years, before that, she looked into insurance claims; she was no stranger to investigations. Unfortunately, no matter how familiar she was with the process, it never got easier to deal with the frustration when faced with a dead end.

She stood, stretching her back. Her laptop was open to a list of students enrolled in all the magical schools of the area, all the way to Boston, but so far, she had no luck finding Maggie or Lacey.

Or rather, she has had too much luck. There were dozens of people with one of those names, far more than she had expected to find. None of them were named Rizzoli, though, and as such, she had no way to narrow down her list.

Taking out her phone, she glanced at the last message she had sent Adam Parker, telling him she might have a lead.

"Sorry, Detective," she muttered as she typed a new message. "Didn't turn out anything."

She sent it, then watched her phone, feeling a little ridiculous. So far, her time in Turtle Bay had undoubtedly given her a new start, one she hadn't expected. But she sensed that a friendship could develop between her and the detective.

Annie could use a friend in this new time of her life.

"No point in sitting around, letting myself think about the divorce," she said—it had been several days since she had last thought of her ex-husband's name. Keeping busy certainly helped with that. "Maybe I should take a break from human hunting and go house-hunting instead!"

She laughed at her joke, pulled on a jacket, and then headed outside. A gentle wind was coming off the bay today, and as she walked, she admired the buildings. She had just turned onto Montgomery Street and spotted a For Sale sign when her phone rang.

It was Adam. Her heart did this strange little flip in her chest.

"Hello?"

"Miss Archer. Could you come down to the station? I have some new information that might help you on your side of the arrangement." Adam sounded amused when he referred to this as an arrangement.

She supposed it was better than the Detective thinking she was out of line and stepping on his toes. *Oh no, I can't start thinking in cliches.*

"I'm on my way, Detective," she said.

With one last longing look at the *For Sale* sign, she hurried back to her new accommodations. It was a little short-term rental cottage on the beach. Nice enough to spend a while in, but it didn't have the makings of a home. It certainly wasn't as lovely as Nikki's place had been... although Nikki's place really was too luxurious for her wants.

It gave her a place to work and sleep, though; that was all that really mattered.

On impulse, Annie took a longer route to Adam's office; she drove down Montgomery Street and slowed outside of the house that was being sold. She knew this was the place she wanted when she laid eyes on it. She could almost see herself in the front yard, bent over a raised herb bed.

She thought I would have to contact a realtor and make an offer as soon as this case was over. A grin blossomed over her face.

Adam was waiting for her in the lobby when she arrived at the police station. He led her down the short hallway to his office, holding the door open for her.

"Thank you," she said as she stepped in.

A haggard-looking man in a worn suit sat in a chair next to the desk. Adam pulled a chair out for Annie before he rounded his desk and sat down.

"Annie, this is Erik Fields. He's Nikki's lawyer," Adam gestured to the man in the suit. "Mr. Fields, this is Miss Archer. She's a witch like Mrs. Rizzoli was."

Mr. Fields gave Annie a kind smile. "I'm very pleased to meet you, Miss Archer. Please don't be alarmed, but I know a lot about you. When you applied to rent from Mrs. Rizzoli, she had me look into you. She was always cautious about who she would rent to and told me more than once that you were ideal. I'm just so very sorry you never got to know her."

Annie was touched by his genuineness. "Thank you. And I've very sorry that you lost her. I might not have known her for long, but she seemed like such a lovely person."

"She was," Mr. Fields agreed. He cleared his throat and pulled a file of papers from his briefcase. "Now, as to why I'm here. Detective Parker contacted me, asking about Mrs. Rizzoli's son, Howard."

"Let me guess; you haven't been able to contact him," Annie said.

Mr. Fields looked surprised. "That's exactly right. I haven't. He moved from the address he last gave Mrs. Rizzoli, and his number was no longer in use; I have a private investigator looking for him now. How did you know?"

"It fits in with my theory," she explained. "Mrs. Rizzoli didn't leave him anything in her will, correct?"

"She didn't," Mr. Fields said, still looking surprised. "You see, she and her son were badly estranged because of how he treated his high school girlfriend."

Annie nodded, sitting up straighter. This was all fitting in with her thoughts. "Because he got his girlfriend pregnant and then dumped her right away?"

"How do you know this?" Mr. Fields asked in amazement.

"It's a guess," Annie said, "but it was the only thing that made sense. Nikki told me that the amethyst was passed from parent to child, but she didn't have any daughters. The name on the back of the necklace was the current owner's name. But not only were there two names, neither of them was Nikki's."

Adam leaned forward. "So you figured it was the shared name of Maggie and Lacey because the necklace should belong to the son, but since he was disowned, it then moved to the next in line—the grandchild."

"Exactly," Annie said.

"But why was it in your room? Why wouldn't it have remained where Nikki left it?" Adam asked.

Annie tapped her chin thoughtfully. "That's the one thing I haven't figured out yet."

"When did Nikki remove Howard from her will?" Adam asked, looking at Mr. Fields again.

He checked his papers. "It was made official only a few months ago. Everything she has goes to Margaret and Lacey Lansbury."

"Lansbury," Annie repeated under her breath. That name sounded familiar.

"And he has had no contact with his mother since then?" Adam pressed.

His eyes were gleaming, and Annie knew he had something. She got closer to him, more excited.

"Not that I'm aware of," Mr. Fields said.

"And yet I have a traffic ticket for a vehicle registered under his name here in Turtle Bay. So, he did come here recently. Perhaps he discovered his inheritance was going to his old girlfriend and daughter."

"He could use the necklace to establish his place in the inheritance if it bore his name," Annie said. "But it didn't—"

Adam nodded once. "Which means that his only access to Nikki's wealth—"

"Is through them," Annie breathed.

As they started at each other, a thrill of triumph washed through Annie. She could have hugged the detective at that moment. Now, more than ever, she was absolutely sure that Howard Rizzoli had killed his mother.

Which presented a problem.

Several problems, actually; How would they prove it? How would they find it? And did this mean that Maggie and Lacey were in danger now?

"We have to find them," she breathed.

Mr. Fields cleared his throat. "I don't have any contact information for them."

"Don't worry—I have lots of connections in the witch community," Annie said. She stood up, already knowing exactly who to call and what to say. "I can find them. Get ready to go, Detective. We're going to solve this case before you know it!"

CHAPTER SIX

IT WAS a three-hour drive before Annie and Adam pulled into the driveway of a farm. The house desperately needed repair; the siding having lost its paint long ago. The roof had been repaired in various patches, like a quilt. The old pickup truck sitting under a torn tarp wasn't in excellent repair, either.

"My goodness," Annie murmured, her heart hurting to see the state of this place. "This has to be a generational farm. Look over there," she pointed into a half-collapsed shed. "Do you see that bike? It's got to be at least fifty years old."

"You're right," Adam said with a slight nod.

Annie turned to him, surprised. "You know antiques?"

"Not really," Adam admitted. "But I can tell you that Maggie's family has been on this property for a very long time." At Annie's surprised look, he laughed. "Hey, I do my research as well."

She couldn't help but laugh as well. They got out of Adam's car and headed toward the farmhouse. Before they even got to the door, it opened. A woman in her mid-thirties stepped out, her dark eyes flitting between them warily. Annie couldn't help but flinch. While she didn't dress lavishly by any means, she felt too flashy for the state of this farm.

"Hello," the woman called. "Can I help you?"

"Maggie Lansbury?" Adam asked. At the woman's nod, he handed her his identification. "I'm Detective Adam Parker, and this is Miss Annie Archer. Do you know a woman named Nikki Rizzoli?"

Maggie shivered. "Come on in, Detective, Miss Archer. I have a feeling this is going to be a long discussion."

"Actually, if you don't mind, I'd like to talk with Miss Lansbury alone," Annie said quickly, turning to Adam. She gave him a significant look; Maggie was already clearly on edge; it might be easier to get her to cooperate if it was just Annie there.

Adam nodded. Annie couldn't stop herself from beaming at him. It still surprised her at how easily they had fallen into this partnership. Part of her didn't want to solve the case, so they could keep working together.

"Do you mind, Miss Lansbury?" Adam asked.

"Um… no. It should be fine." Maggie seemed to attempt a smile but failed miserably.

Adam tipped his hat to her and headed back toward the car. Seemingly hesitant, Maggie led Annie into the house. The interior was much better kept than the exterior. The flooring looked relatively new, and everything was spotless.

"This is my daughter, Lacey," Maggie said once they were in the living room. Lacey sat on a reclining armchair with a book.

Annie recognized the title. "You're taking potion charms, are you?" she asked politely.

Lacey looked up, her eyes widening. "How do you know?"

"I'm a witch myself," Annie told her, smiling. "Potions are my specialty."

"Mine too," Lacey said shyly.

Maggie took a seat, rubbing her hands on her knees. "The detective said something about Nikki?"

Annie folded her hands in her lap. "I'm very sorry to tell you that Nikki passed away a little over a week ago. Did you keep in touch with her at all after…?"

"After Howard and I separated, you mean?" Maggie's tone was stressed, and she glanced at Lacey, who was watching in confusion.

Annie chose her following words carefully. She didn't know how much Maggie had told Lacey, after all. "Nikki had a necklace in her possession. An amethyst necklace."

"That was passed down in her family, I know," Maggie said, looking away. "When I found out I was pregnant, she told me one day it would be my child's. But then Howard and I decided to see one another no longer, and… well, I fell out of touch with Nikki. Are you here to give her the necklace?"

"No, I'm afraid not. It was stolen; we think Howard may have taken it. Has he gotten in touch with you at all lately?"

Maggie pressed her lips together tightly.

Annie waited a moment before she leaned forward. "Lacey was born at 5:30 in the afternoon, wasn't she? And you were born close to six."

Maggie let out a heavy breath and nodded.

"The necklace, when I saw it, had your names inscribed. Nikki disowned her son for what he did to you, Maggie. You have inherited everything Nikki had. Her property, her money, everything. And…" She glanced at Lacey, uncertain. Should she really tell a teenage girl that her father may have killed her grandmother.

Before she could make up her mind, the door burst open. Annie jumped to her feet, whirling to face the man who entered. He lifted his lip in a silent snarl, his hands clenching around something that glinted in the light.

"So, you're the nosy woman who found the necklace before I could remove my mother's protective spells on it," he sneered as his gaze swept up and down Annie. "If I had known you were in the house that night…."

Annie's throat went dry.

Maggie pulled Lacey to her feet and put herself between her ex and her daughter. "What do you want, Howard? Why are you here? What did you do?"

Howard looked at her. "I'm here to get what belongs to me. My mother should have left everything to me. Everything. Especially this!"

He lifted his hands. The amethyst necklace shone in the light. A powerful aura pulsed in the air; the same sort of power Annie had felt from it before. Only now, the power was magnified. Maddie and Lacey gasped; they could sense it, too.

It's more potent because it's in the presence of its rightful owners, Annie realized.

"You killed her," Annie accused, pointing at him. "You killed her for that power."

Howard flinched. "No. No, I didn't kill her! She killed herself. I went to talk to her. Just talk. She was acting crazy, slurring her speech, talking nonsense. She pulled the necklace out and accused me of trying to steal from her. Steal! I wasn't stealing it; it belongs to me. My birthright!"

"It wasn't yours. She decided whom it went to next, and you proved yourself unworthy," Annie said, edging away from Maddie and Lacey.

"It is mine," Howard insisted. "But it's got a charm on it. It can only be worn by the person whose name is on it... I didn't believe her. I wanted her to give it to me. She was walking away, telling me she was too tired to deal with me. I put the necklace on her because it wasn't true. She was lying to me. It tightened..."

He swallowed hard, his face going pale. Maggie gasped, and Lacey clung to her mother.

"Howard... she was under a sleeping potion," Annie said.

"Wh-what?"

"She accidentally put a sleeping potion in our dinner. She wasn't trying to ignore you... she just couldn't stay awake."

Howard stared at her for a long moment before his expression darkened. "You killed her!"

He lunged, holding the necklace out as though to wrap it around Annie's neck.

In the next moment, Adam tackled him to the ground. Howard yelled and thrashed, but Adam quickly had him handcuffed. The amethysts pulsed with power, just out of Howard's reach. Annie snatched the necklace up and held it at arm's length.

"Good timing," Annie said gratefully to Adam.

He pulled Howard to his feet and smiled at her. "I had to wait until we had a confession, didn't I?" His expression sobered. "Are you three all right?"

Annie nodded as she handed the necklace to Maggie.

"Annie, I'm going to need that for evidence," Adam said.

"It's not yours to keep from them," Annie told him ruefully. "I can help you go through the proper channels with the coven, but this is a family artifact. Besides, you have a confession from this... man," she said, scowling at Howard.

Adam considered her for a moment before he nodded. "Very well. I'm not going to fight over this. Come on, Mr. Rizzoli. You're under arrest for the murder of Nicole Rizzoli. You have the right to remain silent...."

Several weeks later, Annie stopped by Adam's office again. She brought a basket of fruit as a thanks for letting her help him with the case. Adam was pleased to see her and accepted the gift heartily.

"So, what's going to happen with Howard now?" she asked, sitting in one chair near his desk.

"Thanks to you, Maggie, and Lacey, we have enough witnesses to his confession to lock him away for the rest of his life for killing his mother and threatening you," Adam told her. He leaned against his desk. "Mr. Fields told me everything is legally in order for Maggie and Lacey to inherit. They're going to be well taken care of from now on."

"Good."

Adam admired the basket of fruit. "And what about you, Miss Archer? Are you staying, or has Turtle Bay proven to be too dangerous a place for you?"

"I just closed the sale on the house over on Montgomery Street this morning," Annie chirped. "I like it here."

A smile spread over Adam's face. "Good! I was hoping you'd stay."

"You were?" Annie looked pleased.

"I've never been able to close a case so easily. It's been nice working with you. And I feel we'll have many more adventures together, Little Witch."

EPILOGUE

MONTY STOPPED TYPING. He stared at the pages he'd just written, stacked neatly beside him. They weren't the tale he had been meaning to write... he threw himself back in his chair and flung a hand over his eyes. This was the story Annie and Adam had been talking about!

You have got to be kidding me, he thought.

All of Annie's new inventory was taken care of by this time. While Winston curled up on Adam's shoulders, she and Adam were drinking coffee and laughing.

Monty frowned, but if the cat liked Adam, he might have some good points after all... Especially considering how the detective adopted the cat without a second thought, despite his own allergies. If only he would be open to Annie about his intentions of courting her!

"So much has changed since those days," Annie mused as she leaned back against the wall. "How many cases have we solved together since then? It's got to be at least a dozen."

"Depends on if you count all the missing pets as 'cases,'" Adam replied. He scratched Winston's ears and smiled at her. "It's been great, though. I'm a lucky man to have you come into my life."

Oh, of course. He's building up to a sudden kiss that—

Monty's brows arched in surprise as Annie pressed herself to her tiptoes and kissed Adam on the cheek. He knew things were different these days but—

But nothing. He put a new sheet of paper into his typewriter and shook his head. Maybe he didn't have to be all so protective of Annie, at that. She had been married once; she knew the wiles of men trying to get their way.

And, if Monty was honest with himself, Detective Parker didn't seem like the sort of man who played the long con game with women.

You had better have honorable intentions, Monty typed. Just a little warning would suffice. He folded the paper into a plane and tossed it to where the two chatted.

Adam's eyes widened as the plane fell to his feet, but it was Annie who picked up the paper. Her eyes narrowed to slits as she looked up at Monty. "What is this about?"

Monty pointed at Adam.

Adam read it, then snorted. He set Winston on the counter behind him. "My intentions?" he repeated. He rolled his eyes. "My intentions are to go get breakfast for Annie—you've forgotten to eat again, haven't you?"

Annie opened her mouth, then closed it. She blushed as she sheepishly nodded.

"There, then. I'll get breakfast, and we can discuss the case I've just been assigned." Detective Adam Parker grinned at Annie.

She beamed back. "Sounds great."

Monty hid a grin as he turned back to his typewriter. He needed something to fill his time as he worked on his Magnus Opus. 'The Annie Archer Mysteries' seemed like just the thing.

The End

Did you enjoy *the Annie Archer Paranormal Mysteries?*
Please consider rating it on Bookbub, Goodreads or your favorite retailer. Reviews help me reach new readers.

Stay tuned for ***Annie Archer Paranormal Mysteries Volume 2.***

Join my newsletter for writing updates, new releases, recipes, giveaways and promotions!

ABOUT THE AUTHOR

Daisy Landish is a romance and contemporary fiction author whose clean and sweet novellas have tugged at readers' heartstrings around the world. When she's not writing love stories, Daisy spends her time reading, hiking at dawn, and riding into the sunset on her horse, Rosebud.

Join Daisy's Newsletter for updates and giveaways!
www.daisylandishromance.com

facebook.com/daisylandishromance
x.com/daisy_landish
instagram.com/daisylandishbooks
amazon.com/author/daisylandish
bookbub.com/authors/daisy-landish
goodreads.com/Daisy_Landish

ALSO BY DAISY LANDISH

Clean Regency Romance

The Lady Series - The Allington Collection

The Lady Series - The Gillingham Collection

The Lady Series - The Blackmore Collection

The Lady Series - The Norrington Collection

Clean Contemporary Romance

Maplewood Grove Series

Love on Spruce Island

Second Chance

Cherry Tree Island

The Wedding Trio

Extra Credit

Counting on the Cowboy

Focusing on the Cowboy

Mistletoe Magic

Grounded at Christmas

Cozy Mysteries

Sophie Brooks Mysteries

Jane and Kennedy Daniels Mysteries

Pine Grove Mysteries

Annie Archer Paranormal Mysteries

Wilma Wade Holiday Mysteries

Mike and Maddie Mysteries

Mystic Moonhaven Mysteries

Sweater Weather: Cozy Mysteries for Fall

Summer Vibes: Cozy Mysteries for Summer

Let it Snow: Cozy Mysteries for Winter

Spring Break: Cozy Mysteries for Spring

www.ingramcontent.com/pod-product-compliance
Lightning Source LLC
Chambersburg PA
CBHW020326260626
47156CB00004B/1400